"I don't ever pla[n] to be penniless."

Kaye didn't realize how defensive she sounded until the words were out.

Brendan raised an eyebrow. "Now I understand why Graham is so attractive to you."

Stubbornly she refused to apologize for her way of thinking. "Romance doesn't last very long when the bills don't get paid," she said, "and there are a lot more important things in marriage than love."

"Name two." There was a cold edge to Brendan's voice.

She looked at him with challenge in her eyes. "Respect," she retorted. "And a feeling of security. And shared goals. That's three—so there. Are you satisfied?"

He was staring at her in disbelief. Then his eyes became so dark that there was no blue left in them. Finally he said, very quietly, "Are you trying to convince me, or yourself, Kaye?"

Leigh Michaels has spent the past three years looking for her dream house, a search that sometimes left her feeling—much like Kaye Reardon—that there was "no place like home." Leigh and her husband have recently moved, and she says the long delay was worth it. "Not only is the house perfect," she adds, "but the search gave me all sorts of ideas for romances!"

Books by Leigh Michaels

HARLEQUIN ROMANCE

2657—ON SEPTEMBER HILL
2734—WEDNESDAY'S CHILD
2748—COME NEXT SUMMER
2806—CAPTURE A SHADOW
2830—O'HARA'S LEGACY
2879—SELL ME A DREAM
2951—STRICTLY BUSINESS
2987—JUST A NORMAL MARRIAGE
2997—SHADES OF YESTERDAY

HARLEQUIN PRESENTS

702—KISS YESTERDAY GOODBYE
811—DEADLINE FOR LOVE
835—DREAMS TO KEEP
876—TOUCH NOT MY HEART
900—LEAVING HOME
1004—THE GRAND HOTEL
1028—BRITTANY'S CASTLE
1049—CARLISLE PRIDE
1068—REBEL WITH A CAUSE
1107—CLOSE COLLABORATION
1147—A NEW DESIRE

Don't miss any of our special offers. Write to us at the following address for information on our newest releases.

Harlequin Reader Service
901 Fuhrmann Blvd., P.O. Box 1397, Buffalo, NY 14240
Canadian address: P.O. Box 603,
Fort Erie, Ont. L2A 5X3

NO PLACE
LIKE HOME

Leigh Michaels

Harlequin Books

TORONTO • NEW YORK • LONDON
AMSTERDAM • PARIS • SYDNEY • HAMBURG
STOCKHOLM • ATHENS • TOKYO • MILAN

Original hardcover edition published in 1988
by Mills & Boon Limited

ISBN 0-373-03010-X

Harlequin Romance first edition October 1989

CHAPTER ONE

IT WAS a grey and dingy day at the end of February, with low-hanging clouds that threatened snow. In the car park of the shopping plaza, there was little activity. Inside the building that housed the travel agency, there was less. It was Saturday afternoon, and it seemed to Kaye Reardon, as she stared out at the car park, as if there hadn't been a customer all week.

She sighed and turned away from the plate-glass window. 'I always thought,' she said to the woman who was filing her nails at the desk closest to the door, 'that this kind of weather was the best there could be for travel agents. I can't think of one person who wouldn't want to get out of Henderson, Illinois right now. But where are they all? They should be standing in line to buy tickets!'

Emily Norton blew an enormous bubble with her wad of chewing gum and popped it loudly. 'Everybody who can afford to go anywhere has already gone.'

'That's true enough,' Kaye admitted. 'I suppose if I had any extra cash I'd be in the Caribbean right now, too.'

'No, you wouldn't,' Emily said unkindly. 'Any time you have an extra dime it goes into your savings account. I've never seen anyone as stingy as you are, Kaye——'

'I'm careful with my money.'

'Isn't that what I said?'

Kaye ignored her. 'I'd be lying on the beach and soaking up the sun in my new swimsuit,' she added dreamily, 'which is really the most gorgeous thing I have ever owned. I got it in a sale last week.' And, she reminded herself, even the sale price had been extravagant. A tiny frown creased her forehead. It wasn't as if she had really needed that swimsuit——

Emily seemed to read her mind. 'If it was in a sale, you can't take it back, so you might as well stop worrying and enjoy it. Besides,' she suggested slyly, 'maybe Graham will ask you to sneak off with him for a spring vacation. He can certainly afford a week in San Juan or Acapulco.'

'Emily, Graham is not the type to suggest sneaking off anywhere——'

'I know,' Emily said regretfully. 'Of course you're right. But I have this conviction that no man can really be as damned straight and respectable as Graham Forrest seems. Now if he was just a tiny bit of a rake, I wouldn't worry so much about what he might be hiding——'

'Does that account for your divorce?' Kaye asked sweetly. 'Your husband wasn't quite rakish enough to please you?'

Emily winced. 'All right, Kaye Reardon,' she said. 'That's playing dirty. My husband was a rat, and everybody—including his second wife, the poor girl—knows it. But Graham is a different story. If he had just the tiniest hint of sin about him, he'd be perfect. He's certainly got a stable job, and more than enough money to be eligible. And there aren't many bachelors his age running around. But——'

'I don't know why you think respectability is such a dreadful thing, Emily.'

'I don't, exactly. It's just so dull——'

'And comfortable,' Kaye pointed out. 'And after the way I grew up, being dragged from one place to another and never quite sure where my next meal was coming from——'

Emily sighed. 'I suppose you have a point. But isn't there a happy medium, Kaye? You've dated some very nice young men. To marry Graham——'

'Aren't you getting ahead of yourself?' Kaye said sweetly. 'Graham hasn't proposed.'

'Surely you've thought about it, Kaye.'

'Of course I have. If Graham proposes, I'll marry him. If he doesn't, I'll——' She caught herself and changed her serious tone for a lightly mocking one, her big green eyes feigning tragedy. 'I'll just have to get another cat to keep me company on lonely Saturday nights.'

Emily snorted. 'Is he taking you out tonight? Graham, I mean, not Omar the cat.'

Kaye nodded. 'Dinner at Pompagno's.'

Emily thought it over. 'That might be a promising sign. Pompagno's—if one of my dates took me there, I'd know he was serious. But to Graham Forrest it probably doesn't mean a thing. What is it the Chicago papers call him? The baby-food tycoon?'

Kaye couldn't bring herself to resent Emily's slightly acid tone; Emily was right, after all. Pompagno's was expensive, and for most people in Henderson an evening there was a special occasion. To Graham, as the president and majority stockholder of the largest producer of baby foods in the Midwest, the bill would be no more a matter of concern than would a hamburger and a milkshake at a downtown diner.

'You've been dating him for months,' Emily pondered. 'I wonder what's holding him up?'

Kaye shrugged. 'I don't read minds.'

The telephone rang, and Emily put her nail file down, tossed her bubble gum into the bin, and reached for it.

'Gulliver's Travel,' she said, making a face at Kaye as she said the words.

It was a ridiculous name for a business, Kaye thought. She winced every time she said it, herself. But Marilyn, the owner of the agency, had what she fondly called a poetic turn of mind, and so Gulliver's Travel it was.

She had worked at the agency for just a few months, learning the travel business, and she had quickly grown to like planning itineraries and smoothing out details. But she hadn't expected to be quite so jealous of every customer who came in to make arrangements for a vacation. Puerto Rico, Paris, Rome, Tokyo—they were just names to Kaye, pinpoints on a map, and likely to remain so for a long time to come. Unless Graham Forrest proposed to her.

It isn't shameful to think of things like that when I consider getting married, she told herself. Graham can afford all of those things I long for—luxurious travel, and really nice clothes, and pretty things to surround me. It isn't awful of me to consider a man's financial standing; I'm just being realistic.

Not that she was petty enough to consider only money. If she didn't like and respect Graham, she would never think of marrying him, no matter how many millions the Forrest baby-food empire had amassed over the years. And it would not be the end of the world if Graham never proposed, she told herself. She had been responsible for herself, when it came right down to it, for most of her life; she wasn't afraid to be on her own. But life could be so much *nicer* if there was a little extra cash... And cash was something Graham Forrest had plenty of.

Besides, she told herself, Graham was so steady, so dependable—so unlike her father.

Emily was reading airline schedules from the computer screen into the telephone. I should be working on the arrangements for that tour group that Marilyn is taking up into Michigan next autumn to admire the leaves, Kaye told herself. There are just a few details left to take care of. But who can think creatively about autumn leaf colour on a grimy day in February, when it feels as if it will always be winter?

The second telephone line rang, and Kaye rushed back to her desk to answer it.

It was a man's voice, deep and confident. 'Kaye?'

'Hello, Graham.'

'I know it's very late notice, but my mother wondered if you and I could join her for cocktails this evening. She's just got back from the south of France, and she'd like to meet you.'

Kaye's heart started to thud so hard against her ribs that she was sure it must sound to him as if there was a jackhammer operating in the car park. She knew Mrs Forrest by sight, of course; everyone who lived in Henderson did. But she had never met the woman face to face.

'I'd be delighted,' she said. 'But it's my night to work late. The agency doesn't close till six——' She sent a pleading look at Emily, who shook her head regretfully.

'Mother will understand if we're a little late, I'm sure,' Graham said briskly, 'and our dinner reservation isn't until nine. I'll pick you up at quarter to seven, Kaye, at your apartment.'

'Good news?' Emily asked the instant that Kaye put the telephone down. 'Or tragedy? It's hard to tell from your face.'

'I'm not sure. Graham's mother wants to meet me. She's asked me to cocktails——'

'And that must mean Graham is really serious. Well, I wish you the best. If my son didn't have a basketball game tonight, I'd stay late and let you rush off to make yourself even more gorgeous than usual. What are you going to wear?'

'The dress I was planning to wear to Pompagno's will just have to be good enough.'

Emily giggled. 'Unless you want to put on the famous new swimsuit,' she said. 'Seeing you in that should certainly make up Graham's mind for him!'

When Emily left at five, there hadn't been a phone call or a walk-in customer for two hours, and it had started to snow. 'I wouldn't mind staying,' Emily said, 'if only Brad didn't have this game tonight——'

'It's certainly not your fault that it's my weekend to work late,' Kaye said, and crossed her fingers in the hope that she might be able to sneak out a few minutes early.

At a quarter to six, the door opened, and a large-boned woman in a fake-fur coat came in, surrounded by a bubble of frigid air. 'My goodness, it's awful out there,' she said. 'I should think you'd want to be getting home.'

Kaye smiled coolly. 'We'll be open for another few minutes. May I help you with something?'

'What have you got on Hawaii?'

Six months at the agency had taught Kaye that the most unlikely-looking people were often the ones who went first class and didn't complain about the price. And this woman, she thought with impatience, certainly looked unlikely! 'When were you thinking of going?' she asked. 'And for how long? We have some package tours available through March——'

'Oh, I'm not going,' the woman laughed. 'It's for my boy. He's got to write a report for school, and I figured you'd have a lot of stuff.'

Kaye bit her tongue. 'Perhaps the library would be a better source for the kind of information he needs,' she said frostily.

'It's closed,' the woman pointed out. 'I've always wanted to go to Hawaii. I thought I'd like to read about it with him.'

There was a wistful note in her voice, and Kaye was heartily ashamed of herself for her impatience. There isn't much difference between us, she thought; we both long for sun and sand, and Gulliver's Travel might be the closest we'll ever get to our dreams. 'I'll be happy to give you some brochures,' she said, more gently. 'The pictures will be useful, at least.'

It was ten after six when she locked the door of the agency behind her, and there was already an inch of snow covering her old car. She brushed it off with the sleeve of her coat, discovered that there was ice underneath, and groaned. 'Dammit,' she said aloud. 'Wouldn't you think that one single thing would go my way tonight?' She was only ten blocks from home. She could drive the distance in five minutes, but it would take half an hour to clear off all the windows.

She scratched out a ragged gap on the windscreen and a tiny circle on the rear window and defiantly got into the car. There is no point in cleaning it all off, she told herself. It will just get covered up again as soon as I'm home. I will drive very slowly and very carefully, and nothing will happen.

That was what she was thinking as she put the car into reverse and backed, very slowly and carefully, directly into the front corner of a small car that had just pulled into the plaza car park.

The shriek of metal against metal and the blare of a car horn blended into a horrible squeal that scraped

Kaye's nerves. She stepped hard on the brake and sat clutching the wheel and shaking.

A car door slammed. I have to get out and face the other driver, she thought miserably. I am completely at fault, and I wouldn't be surprised if I end up in court over this——

She slid out into the snow. The other driver was bending over the corner of the car she had hit, inspecting the damage. She sneaked a look—he was definitely male, not particularly tall or big, but certainly nothing to tangle with, and—if her instinct was worth anything at all—he was furious.

One glance at his car and she was certain. It was small, and not new, but it was well-kept, and it was polished to a gleam, at least where the snow wasn't hiding the finish. And it was apparent, even to Kaye, that it would never be quite the same again.

If that was my car and he had hit it, she thought, I'd kill him right here in the car park. No questions asked.

The driver straightened up and turned to look at her. He was rubbing a leather-gloved hand along his jaw, and Kaye eyed it with uncertainty. Her first impression had been correct; he wasn't terribly tall, but he was solidly built and compact, and beside her own slender five-foot-three, he was quite large enough to be threatening.

'Wouldn't you think,' he said finally, 'that the cosmic forces would at least let me make the last payment on it before it gets smashed?'

Kaye blinked. Whatever she had expected, it hadn't been that. Profanity would not have surprised her; she would have stood there meekly and listened while he lambasted her character, feeling that she deserved every word of it. But this mildness—somehow, it was even scarier than threats would have been.

'I'm very sorry,' she ventured. 'I was in a hurry, you see.'

'Yes, I gathered that you must have been.' He didn't sound interested. His eyes flicked over the back of her car, assessing its age. 'Might I be allowed to ask if you carry insurance on that thing?'

'Of course I do!' Shock was catching up with her. 'And you don't need to be sarcastic about it!' she added irrationally.

He had bent over his car again; he looked up when her voice cracked, and said, 'Surely you aren't suggesting that I'm the one who caused this accident?' Huge snowflakes were dusting his bare head, starkly white against his dark hair.

Kaye fought back tears and said huskily, 'I'm sorry for yelling at you. Of course you're not to blame.'

'Good. I'm glad we agree on that much. If I may have your name and the necessary insurance information, I'll let you be on your way to whatever was so important.'

She recited it woodenly, and he unbuttoned his dark wool overcoat and reached for a small notebook from an inside pocket. The leather gloves he wore made it hard to write, and he dropped his pen once. She braced herself for an outburst then, but he only stooped to pick it up from the snow and said, 'Kaye Reardon,' spelling it back to her.

She nodded. 'I work at Gulliver's.'

'I see. I'll get estimates of the cost to repair the damage, and I'll call your insurance company. You'd better do the same.'

She looked at her own car. 'I think it only scratched the bumper.'

'These big cars are built like tanks,' he agreed. She looked at him suspiciously, but he didn't sound sarcastic. 'Nevertheless, it might be wise to have it checked out. Here's my card, in case you need to reach me.'

She took it in fingers that felt numb from the cold. 'I'm awfully sorry,' she mumbled. 'I'll make sure it's fixed as good as new.'

He shrugged and looked down at the crumpled fender. 'I doubt that's going to be possible.'

'If it was mine,' she said honestly, 'I'd be furious.'

'What good would that do me? Apart from keeping me warm, perhaps. And speaking of warmth, why don't you get back in your car and pull it forwards a couple of feet? We're blocking traffic, what little there is of it.'

She looked up at him for a long instant. The snow had formed a solid crust over his dark hair and was falling in swirls against the glaring headlights of his car. She wondered what colour his eyes were; it was impossible to tell with the light coming from behind him.

'Kaye Reardon,' he said, and for the first time there was a trace of impatience in his voice, 'until you move your car, I can't move mine. Now I'd love to be a gentleman and stand here in the snow all evening with you, but I do have a date to keep——'

She jumped a little, and thought, What an idiot you are, Kaye! You've got a date, too—— 'Oh,' she said. 'I'm——'

'I know,' he said. 'You're sorry.' He ushered her to her car and opened the driver's door.

She let the car creep forwards a couple of feet to clear the path for him, and then climbed out again with her ice scraper. No matter how long it took, she vowed, or how late she was, she wasn't driving anywhere until she could see through every square inch of glass.

His little car had stopped a few feet away, and the door slammed. 'Here,' he said, taking the scraper out of her hand. 'Let me do that.'

'Thanks,' she muttered.

'I'm not really doing you a favour,' he said, 'as much as I'm trying to do a good deed for every other driver on the road.' He smiled down at her. 'They can use all the help they can get.'

'And you didn't even get his name?' Graham looked worried, and that was unusual.

'He gave me his business card,' Kaye said. 'But I didn't even glance at it at the time, and when I got home and looked for it, I couldn't find it anywhere. I must have dropped it in the car park.'

'Careless, Kaye. That was very careless. You don't even know how to reach him, and you have no idea what kind of person he is.'

'He seemed a pretty restrained sort to me,' she said mildly. 'I had just put a huge crease in his car, and he didn't even yell at me.'

Graham frowned, but he didn't say any more. Kaye was glad. She hadn't intended to tell him about the accident, but he'd been waiting outside her apartment when she had finally got home, and she had had to explain why she was so late. She had changed her clothes in less than five minutes, run a brush through her long blonde hair, thanking heaven for natural curls, and reflected that she wasn't nervous any more about meeting his mother—at least, not much.

The security guard in the lobby of the apartment complex waved them through with a cheerful greeting, and the glass lift whisked them through the five-storey atrium lobby up to the penthouse floor.

'It's beautiful,' Kaye said, with a catch in her voice. 'I never would have dreamed all this could come out of an old warehouse.'

'I know,' Graham said cynically. 'No one else did, either, except for my mother.'

'It was her idea?' Kaye didn't know why that should have startled her.

A man in severe formal garb opened the door. 'Good evening, Mr Graham,' he said. He took Kaye's coat, seeming to pretend that it was mink instead of mere wool, and ushered them into a long living-room with a grand piano at one end and the curtains pulled back to reveal a stunning view of the city below, spread out along the frozen shores of Lake Henderson.

'How lovely!' Kaye exclaimed. 'I had no idea this city could look so wonderful!'

'You don't like living in Henderson?' It was a woman's gentle voice, and Kaye turned to face Claudia Forrest as the older woman rose from a chair beside the windows. She was tiny, all blue and white, with enormous sapphire eyes and soft silver hair.

'Oh, of course I do, but——' Kaye stumbled to a halt, and Claudia laughed, a tinkling trill.

'The city does look prettier from up here, doesn't it? Graham will get you whatever you like to drink, and then you'll come and sit by me, dear, and we'll chat. I'm so glad you could come tonight.'

There was no one else in the room; Kaye realised belatedly that Graham had not said this was to be a party. I really am on trial, she thought, and swallowed hard.

But Claudia was chatting gently. 'I never thought I'd end my days living in a warehouse,' she said. 'Graham's father would have been horrified, I'm sure, but I think it's something of a joke. After all, I heard about baby food morning, noon, and night all the years we were married—what is so strange about living where the tons of oatmeal boxes were stored?'

Kaye giggled. 'Do you mean—here?' She gestured at the elegant room with its cream-coloured carpeting, pastel furniture and striking art.

'Here,' Claudia Forrest said. 'It nearly broke my heart when Graham built the new warehouse out on the edge of town. This building held such memories.'

'It was the only practical thing to do, Mother.' He put a delicate crystal wineglass into Kaye's hand.

'Practical,' Claudia said. 'Sometimes I wonder, Graham, if you will ever realise that being impractical is sometimes much more fun.'

'Also, much less profitable. You'll never get back the money you spent on this place, Mother. You simply can't charge enough rent in a city like Henderson to recover your investment.'

Claudia shrugged. 'If it amuses me, what does the money matter? But let's not quarrel in front of our guest.' Claudia's voice was crisp. In the next hour, she drew Kaye out, asking about her job, her family.

'I haven't any family left,' Kaye said. 'My mother died when I was a baby, and my father several years ago.'

'You're very young to be all alone,' Claudia murmured. The sapphire eyes were hypnotic, and Kaye fought down the sudden, irrational desire to say, I've always been alone. But she couldn't say things like that to a woman she scarcely knew. She couldn't confide those details to Graham's mother, who would probably forbid her son to ever see this young woman again.

It was all in the past, anyway. The fact that Kaye's father had been a less than reliable parent and provider, that they had lived on the thin edge of poverty, didn't matter in the least. It wasn't as if he'd been a criminal, after all, Kaye told herself stoutly. A black sheep, perhaps, but from a good enough family nevertheless,

one even Claudia Forrest couldn't object to. And so she
smiled and talked of ordinary things.

On the way to Pompagno's, Graham looked across at
Kaye, cleared his throat, and said, 'My mother likes you
very much.'

'I'm glad,' Kaye said. 'I like her, too.'

He gave a self-conscious little cough. 'I intended to
wait a while to ask this—perhaps order a bottle of
champagne at Pompagno's—but that's rather public,
don't you think?'

'Public for what?' Kaye asked. Her heart was beating
a little faster than usual. She was afraid to look at him;
instead, she looked straight ahead to where the highway
turned away from the frozen shore of Lake Henderson.

'Will you become my wife, Kaye?'

She closed her eyes tightly. A strange little pain
rocketed through her, tingling clear to her fingertips,
followed by a tidal wave of relief that threatened to drown
her. This, then, was what love really felt like, she
thought. She'd simply been terrified to let herself feel it
before, afraid that Graham might not want to marry her
at all.

I hadn't realised, she thought, just what rigid controls
I was putting on my feelings.

'Kaye?' he asked quietly. 'I'm sorry if it sounds as if
I needed my mother's approval before I proposed to you.
But you do understand why I waited, don't you?'

'Of course,' she said quietly. 'It wouldn't be very
pleasant for any of us if your mother and I couldn't
stand each other. It was only sensible to wait till she got
home. Graham, thank you. Of course I'll marry you.'

There, she thought. It's all decided. And I am thrilled.

He smiled at her, and patted her gloved hand where
it lay on the leather upholstery. 'Thank you, my dear,'
he said gently. 'We will be quite happy together, I'm

sure.' He laughed a little. 'And Mother will be delighted. She's thought for a long time that a man in my position shouldn't be single. The baby-food business, I mean. She keeps hinting that it's time to put a picture of a new Forrest baby on the labels.'

He's blushing, Kaye thought in astonishment. Graham is actually embarrassed.

'All in due time, of course,' he added hastily. 'There is no hurry about it—no hurry at all.' He hesitated, and added warily, 'I should have asked about your views on the subject, of course.'

She wondered idly what would happen if she said indignantly that she absolutely refused to ever have a child, and then scolded herself for letting the relief of the moment make her get silly and half-hysterical. How could such a crazy thought ever have come into her head, anyway?

'I haven't ever given it much thought,' Kaye said. 'But I've always hoped to have children some day. I'd like several, I think. I was an only child, and it was very lonely.'

He laughed again, with a little relief. 'Well, at least there's no fighting when there's only one,' he said.

He turned the car over to the doorman outside Pompagno's, and took Kaye's arm to usher her inside. 'Kaye, my dear,' he said. 'I'm honoured that you've put your trust in me. I promise you will never want for anything.'

It was only then that she realised it. Neither of them had said anything about love.

CHAPTER TWO

MONDAY morning at the travel agency was not often busy, but it seemed to Kaye that everyone in town had cabin fever after the snowy weekend at home, and immediately started planning to leave. She and Emily were both occupied for most of the morning, and it was nearly noon before Emily pushed her chair back, picked up her coffee mug, and said, 'How did you get along with Graham's mama Saturday night?'

'Just wonderfully, thank you.' Kaye addressed an envelope, rolled it out of the typewriter, put in a cruise-ship brochure, and dropped it into the outgoing mail. She couldn't resist giving Emily a jolt. 'The wedding will be next summer some time.'

Emily choked and sputtered. 'Don't do that to me,' she begged. 'I can't take practical jokes of that sort.'

'It isn't a practical joke. Graham proposed, I accepted, and we'll set a date as soon as I find a house for us to buy.' Kaye propped her elbows on her desk and smiled happily across at her co-worker. 'It's real. I'm engaged.'

Emily put the cup down. 'I don't see a ring.'

'Graham hasn't had a chance to get one yet.'

'Do you mean to tell me he didn't even think ahead far enough to buy you a ring?'

'It was only Saturday night that he proposed, Emily——'

'How awfully romantic of him to act so uncertain of your answer,' Emily drawled. 'Or—on the other hand—

how very practical of him to avoid the chance of being stuck with a second-hand diamond.'

'Don't be sarcastic. It's foolish to buy a ring for someone without knowing what she likes——'

'Oh? Do you mean to tell me you're actually going to marry someone who's never bothered to notice whether you prefer simple designs or clusters of glitter? If he has no idea what your taste in jewellery is, Kaye, doesn't it make you wonder what else he doesn't know about you?'

'Emily, if you insist on twisting what I say, I'm going to stop talking to you.'

'Sorry, Kaye. I'm in shock, that's all. So the great man finally went overboard. Champagne and candle-light at Pompagno's, right?'

'Something like that.' Kaye was glad, when she thought about it, that Graham hadn't waited for soft music and romantic candlelight to ask her to marry him. Pompagno's had been crowded on Saturday night, and in those surroundings their private conversation would have stayed private for about fifteen seconds, she thought—approximately as long as it took for one person across the crowded room to jab another in the ribs and say, 'I'll bet Graham Forrest just popped the question!'

'And now you're looking for a house. How domestic.'

Kaye refused to be ruffled. 'We have to have a place to live, Emily. My apartment is certainly too small.'

'No, I can see that would be a problem. It's scarcely large enough for you and the cat.'

'And Graham will want to entertain more, so we might as well buy a house right away.'

'I suppose you're right,' Emily said reluctantly. She came across to Kaye's desk and gave her a hug. 'Best wishes, and all that, you know,' she said. 'I truly do hope that you'll be happy.'

'I know, Emily. And of course I'll be happy. We're
hoping to keep this a bit quiet for a while, though. We'd
like to find a house, and set a date, and then make the
announcement——'

'As soon as you start touring houses in Henderson
Heights, every one of the hundred thousand people in
this city will know what you're up to.'

'I suppose you're right,' Kaye said reluctantly. 'But I
think I'll go first to the estate agent here in the plaza—
it should be a bit easier to keep it mum in a branch office,
don't you think? And it can't be too hard to find what
we're looking for. We made a list yesterday. I'll just give
that to the agent, and she can eliminate the ones we
wouldn't be interested in. I won't have to look at many
houses, I'm sure, before I find the right one.'

'Good luck,' Emily murmured. 'When I was house-
hunting, it never worked that way—but then I was on
a budget. Everything I liked cost twice as much as I could
afford.' She turned to the client who had just walked in
and said, 'Hello, Mrs Meadows. How was the trip to
Italy?'

The telephone rang, and the rush was on again. It
didn't let up till the lunch hour, and when Kaye finally
left the building to go to the delicatessen down the street
it was with a sigh of relief. It was always feast or famine
in the travel business, she thought. Nevertheless, she liked
it much better than the other jobs she'd had. Within the
next few months, she hoped, she would be able to start
guiding a tour now and then. Emily did regularly, and
the owner of the business spent much of her time super-
vising groups. That was where the fun was, Kaye
thought, not in the office reading computer screens.

She paused outside the door of the property sales
office. Lunch first, she wondered, or this? It couldn't
take long to hand her list over and get the process started,

and then she could go and eat her sandwich with a clear conscience. She pushed the door open.

A gorgeous brunette was at the reception desk, flipping pages in a thick album full of photographs of houses. Occasionally she read off an address. Sitting on the corner of the desk with his back to the door was a dark-haired man, notebook and pen in hand, writing down what the woman said. The brunette broke her page-turning rhythm, looked up at Kaye, and said with a smile, 'May we help you?'

The man on the desk turned. 'Oh, no,' he said when he saw Kaye. 'Don't tell me you've dented my car again.'

'I certainly haven't,' she said irritably.

'Well, that's good news. I got the estimates of the cost to repair the damage just this morning, if you'd like to take them to the insurance people.' He slid off the desk.

'I thought you were going to do that.'

'I could, but I assume that is what you came in for. They're in my office.' He strode off. So he worked here, she thought, and wasn't just coming in to check out a house for sale.

He had vanished across a big room, crowded with desks and file cabinets, and into a smaller office. Kaye decided that she could either follow him or stand there and scream in frustration, so she trailed across the big room after him.

He was already tugging a sheaf of papers out of the inside pocket of his overcoat.

'The paperwork on your car is not why I'm here,' she said briskly. 'I want to buy a house.'

'Oh, in that case——' He pushed the papers back into the pocket and waved her to a chair. 'What kind of a house? How large? What part of town? Do you have one to sell before you start looking for a new one? What sort of price range——'

'You can't be a very effective sales person if you don't listen to the customer,' she pointed out coolly.

He grinned at her and leaned back in his chair. 'I'm all ears,' he said. 'It's just that I've found we get somewhere faster if I get some basic information from the client first, like what kind of neighbourhood you prefer and whether you like old houses or new ones——'

'I haven't even said that I want to work with you, Mr——'

'If you don't, why did you come into this particular branch office?'

'Because I didn't know you'd be here!' Kaye snapped.

His eyes, she noticed, were dark blue, and at the moment they were suspiciously bright. 'I gave you my card.'

'I lost it,' she admitted, finally. 'I had no idea you worked here.' Damn, she thought. Why did I have to lose that business card? It's not like me to be so careless, and it's dreadfully embarrassing not even to know his name!

'Somehow,' he murmured, 'that doesn't surprise me. This is apparently not my lucky week. Fortunately, I am always up to a challenge. So tell me about the kind of house you want, Miss Reardon.'

'I think I'd be happier working with someone who will take me seriously.'

'Oh, when it comes to commissions, I take things very seriously,' he assured her. 'If you'd like another copy of my card——'

She took the bit of beige pasteboard with reluctance. His name was Brendan McKenna, it said. That figures, she reflected. He's as Irish as they make them. The dark blue eyes completed that improbable combination of black hair and fair skin that made the Celtic Irish so very attractive. And I'll bet he's kissed the Blarney Stone a time or two as well, she thought; any woman of sense would walk out right now, Kaye Reardon, before he really gets warmed up.

On the other hand, she reminded herself, he had displayed not even a flicker of temper when she had banged up his car, and he had come back to help her get rid of the ice on her windows. If it hadn't been for his assistance, she would never have made it back to her apartment in time to keep her date, and Graham would have gone off in a huff instead of proposing, and she wouldn't be here looking for a house at all—— Perhaps Mr McKenna deserves the benefit of the doubt, she told herself.

'Why do I get the feeling,' he mused, 'that there's a piece of spinach stuck between my front teeth?'

'What?'

'It's the way you're looking at me,' he pointed out.

'I'm sorry.'

'Oh, please, don't let's start that again. If I've passed inspection, perhaps you'll tell me about your house now.'

What difference does it make? Kaye thought. Someone was going to sell her a house and collect the sales commission; why shouldn't it be Brendan McKenna? It would certainly make up to him for the inconvenience she'd caused by battering his car. She passed her list across the desk.

He read the first line and his eyebrows went straight up. '*Five* bedrooms?' he murmured. 'Do you run an orphanage in your spare time, Miss Reardon?'

'My fiancé and I plan to have a family,' she said with composure.

'I see.' It was perfectly bland.

'A small family,' she said, and wished that her fair skin didn't betray her embarrassment so easily. She felt as if her cheeks were burning. 'But we need a guest room as well, and a sewing room, and——'

'My job is to find the bedrooms,' he murmured. 'It's up to you how you use them.'

'We'd prefer to locate in the Henderson Heights area.'

Brendan McKenna looked up from the list. 'Are you certain you and your fiancé know what you're doing, Miss Reardon? Most newlyweds buy a honeymoon cottage somewhere and fix it up——'

'Mr McKenna, my fiancé is Graham Forrest.'

He blinked once. Then he said, with a drawl, 'Well, that does put a different light on matters.'

'I thought it might,' Kaye murmured.

'No wonder you'll need a lot of bedrooms in a hurry. Someone has to eat all that baby food.'

Kaye picked up her handbag and rose. 'I think perhaps it would be best if I went elsewhere, Mr McKenna.'

'If you don't feel comfortable working with me, I wouldn't dream of asking you to stay. But I think you should reconsider—I am just about the best estate agent there is in this city.'

'And modest, too, I see,' she said tartly. She put her handbag down.

'At no extra charge,' he agreed. He looked down at her list. 'Large living and dining-rooms for entertaining—of course. A gourmet kitchen—that goes without saying; caterers are so hard to please these days. On a side street—for the children's safety, yes. Family-room, two-car garage, space for an office or study, and at least two wood-burning fireplaces—tell me, Miss Reardon, don't you want to specify which rooms the fireplaces should be in?'

Kaye refused to react to the sarcastic note in his voice. 'Preferably, in the living-room and the master bedroom suite.'

'I see. Mr Forrest has a thing about fire, does he? It would seem fitting.'

She glared at him. He looked innocent. 'If you don't want my business, Mr McKenna——'

'I never said that. I just meant that this may not be as easy as you seem to think.'

'Mr McKenna, we need a large house, in sound condition, in a good location. For someone with all the talent you've told me you possess, it should be no trouble at all.'

He smiled suddenly, and charm seemed to pour across the room towards her. 'Let's get started. You can read the multiple listing book while I make a couple of phone calls, and we can go look this afternoon.'

'I can't. I have to go back to work. In fact, I'm just on my lunch break——'

'There's one we can look at right now.'

Anxious, isn't he? Kaye thought. He's probably afraid that if I leave here right now, I'll never come back. Well, perhaps this will be the right house, and we can all relax. 'Don't you have other appointments this afternoon?'

'Not a thing.'

That doesn't sound like the best estate agent in town, she thought. She glanced at her watch. 'May I use your telephone?'

'To call Graham to see if he can join us? Sure.' He pushed it across the desk towards her.

'No, as a matter of fact—to call the travel agency. Mr Forrest has given me a completely free hand. He says since the house will be largely my concern, I should be the one to choose it.'

'That's gentlemanly of him,' Brendan McKenna murmured. 'It will be largely your concern, will it?'

'He is a very busy man.'

'I'm certain he is.' It was agreeable and polite.

She felt somehow that she had lost control of the conversation, but before she could figure it out, Marilyn answered the telephone.

'I'll be here, dear,' she said. 'Don't worry about a thing. Emily told me your wonderful news, and if you want to look all afternoon, go ahead—you haven't had a day off in weeks.'

Kaye was startled. She'd always got along well with Marilyn, but the woman had never been quite so effusive before.

Then, as she watched Brendan McKenna flip through the pages of his pocket notebook, things clicked into place. Of course, Kaye thought. I'll be in a position to steer all of Graham's friends to Gulliver's. That's why Marilyn is so anxious for me to be contented just now.

He made a couple of phone calls and then glanced at his watch. 'What I'd like to do this afternoon,' he said, 'is take you to several different kinds of houses, and get an idea which things you like best. I doubt any of them are quite what you're looking for, but——'

'Is that really necessary? It sounds like a waste of time.'

'If we stumble across your dream castle this afternoon, no one could be more pleased than I will be. But if we don't, at least I'll know where to start looking, and what not to show you. We may waste one afternoon, but we'll save lots of time in the long run.'

'All right,' she said doubtfully.

'And I'm certain enough of my eventual success that I'll even buy you lunch before we start,' he added. 'I'll take it out of my commission.'

'Is this another symptom of your humility?' she said.

'That's right. Sales people don't get anywhere without self-confidence.'

'Why don't you bottle some of yours and sell it? You seem to have plenty.' Kaye bit her tongue. Brendan

McKenna seemed to be having an unfortunate effect on her manners. 'I am sorry, Mr McKenna,' she said stiffly. 'That was uncalled for.'

He shrugged it off. 'I think you'd better start calling me Brendan,' he suggested. 'We'll either be the best of buddies by the time this is over, or we will never want to see each other again, but we won't be neutral.'

'I thought we'd already gone far past neutral.'

'After what happened Saturday night, perhaps you're right. It might have been the luckiest car accident of my life. Do you realise that with the commission the seller will pay me when you buy a house, I can buy a whole new car?'

'I'm touched,' Kaye said crisply.

'I thought you would be. Maybe instead of fixing this one, I'll just trade it in on a BMW.' He helped her into her coat.

'I really don't think lunch is such a wonderful idea——' she began.

'Believe me, if you don't eat, by the end of the afternoon you'll wish you had. Cindy,' he said to the gorgeous brunette as they crossed the big office. 'Miss Reardon and I are going to the Wolfpack for lunch and then out to look at houses.'

'The Wolfpack?' Kaye asked. 'That's the name of a restaurant?'

'One of the best in town. I don't know why they call it that—except that you'll see big groups of people there gobbling away as if they're protecting their kill. Let's take my car.'

'I know, you'll feel safer if I'm not driving.'

'I didn't say that.'

'Don't start being diplomatic now.' She stopped to inspect the dent. It looked even worse in daylight. 'I really did put a crease into it, didn't I?'

He nodded. 'The garage said it was lucky you weren't in a real hurry, or I wouldn't be driving it at all.' He unlocked the door. A battered teddy bear was occupying the passenger's seat; he tossed it into the back.

'Oh, please! Now you're really making me feel like a worm.'

'You should. You'll probably have a new car every year from now on, while the rest of us drive old, battered ones.'

She could, she decided. She hadn't thought of things like that before. It was a pleasant thought.

The Wolfpack turned out to be a little bar tucked into a corner of the downtown area. Outside the door, Brendan turned to her and said, 'Perhaps I should have asked if you're the quiche and salad type. If so, we'd better go somewhere else. The Wolfpack leans to a heartier sort of fare.'

'How hearty?' Kaye asked doubtfully.

'Reubens, submarines, hot roast beef with horse-radish——'

'Oh, the kind of thing you can't eat if you don't want anyone to know where you've been.'

'That's the place. They also have the best french fries in Illinois.'

'And I've never heard of it?' I can see why, she thought as they stepped inside. From the pavement, it looked like a seedy dive. Inside, it made no pretensions to style or atmosphere; the table coverings were paper, the chairs looked less than reliable, and the smell was heavenly.

Her reuben was the best she had ever eaten, dripping with sauerkraut and salad dressing. 'You're certainly right about the food,' she said.

He said, modestly, 'I nearly always am. Where do you live now, Kaye?'

'In a studio apartment on Williams Street. Is that important?'

'It might be. We're trying to establish what you really want, so that I show you that and not what I think you should have. What made you choose that apartment? And what do you hate about it?'

She thought it over as she nibbled at the corned beef that peeped out of the edge of her sandwich. 'It was mostly the fact that I could afford the rent,' she said.

'Williams Street is not a luxurious neighbourhood, but neither is it a slum. Let's be serious, please.'

'Sorry. I like it because it has huge windows and it's one big room—all open space for my plants and my cat. I hate it because it's new, so the walls are thin and if the upstairs neighbours make noise it sounds as if I'm living inside a bass drum.' She thought about it. 'I suppose what I'm really saying is that I want an old house, one that has a history to it. One with a classic style.'

'I'm a bit prejudiced towards Victorians myself,' he agreed. 'I suppose it's because I grew up in one. Nevertheless, you'd be amazed at all the people who say they want an old house, and end up buying a new one.'

'I wonder why.'

'Partly because it doesn't sound like a bass drum if there are no upstairs neighbours,' he said gravely. 'And a new house has all kinds of advantages—things like plumbing that isn't half-plugged.'

Kaye shrugged. 'You can't decorate a water pipe at Christmas-time, but you can certainly hang holly on an open staircase.'

He pulled out his notebook and jotted a few words. 'Are you finished with your sandwich?'

Kaye looked regretfully at her plate. 'I give up.'

'Take it home to the cat.'

'Omar is a spoiled baby and a picky eater, so——'
She stared at the sandwich and changed her mind. 'That
corned beef is too good to waste. I'll eat it myself, for
supper.'

Brendan grinned. 'Just don't think that I'm going to
start providing all your meals,' he teased.

'Oh? I thought it was part of the service.'

They looked at eight houses that afternoon. Kaye rejected all of them, and each time she shook her head,
Brendan, with unruffled good humour, merely locked
the front door behind them and drove on to the next.
By the time they got back to the shopping plaza, Kaye
felt as if she had just finished a marathon run.

'If house-hunting is always this tough,' she said,
tossing herself down in the chair beside his desk, 'you
should insist on a medical check-up for clients before
you start.'

'We won't keep up this pace, now that I have an idea
of what you're really looking for.'

'Eight houses, and not a single one of them what I
want.'

'The Georgian brick came close—at least from the
outside.'

'How do you know?' she challenged. 'I said hardly a
word about any of those houses.'

'You have very expressive eyes, my dear,' he said, in
the same tone as if he was the wolf, talking to Little Red
Riding Hood. 'It was in the way you looked at it, before
you went inside and the chopped-up interior made you
feel ill.'

'I was very tactful,' she said defensively.

Brendan laughed. 'Outrage is hard to hide, Kaye. Besides, I felt the same way myself. I can also tell a great
deal by how fast a woman walks through a house. The
slower she walks, the more she likes it—and that one

you raced through as if there was a pack of hounds at your heels.'

'Is that why you dawdled along behind me all the time?'

He nodded. 'It doesn't work that way for men. They're much harder to predict. It's the funniest thing—that's why I prefer to work with women.'

'I'll bet you do,' Kaye murmured.

'For example, I'm not planning to show you any more ranch-style houses, either—am I right?'

She nodded, and shivered at the thought. 'They're so spread out,' she said. 'I'd walk myself to death keeping the place clean!'

'Surely you'll have a housekeeper.'

'I hadn't thought of that.' She considered it, and shook her head. 'I don't think I really want one,' she said. 'I like the idea of playing house under my own roof, with no one to get irate if I want to scrub the kitchen floor in the middle of dinner preparation.'

He was looking at her in astonishment. 'You actually like the idea of scrubbing floors?'

'I don't mind,' Kaye said, feeling a little ridiculous, but determined to stand up for herself. 'And if it was my very own floor, I should think there would be a lot more satisfaction in it.'

'Haven't you ever had a home of your own?'

'Not really, just apartments.' She bit her lip and said stiffly, 'My father and I moved around a lot.'

Brendan looked intrigued, but he didn't comment. He leaned back in his chair. 'Would tomorrow be all right for another session?'

'I don't think I should plan on taking too many afternoons off.'

'Then we'll go after you leave work.'

'You don't mind tying up your own evening?' She was thinking about the battered teddy bear that had been in the front seat of his car, and the child it must belong to.

'It's part of the job.' He saw her out, and as she walked across the car park to her car, she turned and saw him, in the pool of light that was the estate agent's office, sitting on the corner of the desk again and talking to the gorgeous brunette.

Of course he wanted her to find her house soon, she thought. The quicker she found it, the sooner he'd get his money, and the less time he'd have invested in the process.

It's been a long time, she thought, since I've gone shopping for anything, especially without having to worry too much about the price tag. Something tells me this could be a lot of fun—more fun than I've had in years...

CHAPTER THREE

KAYE glanced through the mail while she waited for water to boil so she could make herself a cup of instant coffee. There wasn't much of interest, just a magazine, a letter from a college friend, and a sweepstakes entry form which she dropped into the bin. She had a vague feeling that she'd already been lucky enough for one week, and there was no sense in wasting a stamp to mail a certain loser.

She stirred the coffee crystals into the hot water and carried her cup and her letter to the far corner of the big single room, where Omar the Persian cat watched sleepily from his comfortable nest on a blue cushion at one end of the couch. As soon as she sat down, the cat rose, stretched, yawned, and gracefully swarmed across the couch and into her lap. She stroked the soft white fur and said, 'How would you like to move to a big house, Omar? A house where there's room for all the cushions you want, and you don't have to give up your couch every night so I can unfold it and make it into a bed?'

Omar wrapped his front paws around her neck, then put his nose into her right ear and began to purr throatily. She jerked away from the rumbling, tickling noise and said, 'That's two in favour. I think you can call it a unanimous vote in this household.'

But what house? she thought. Was it going to be so difficult to find just the right house for herself and Graham? Had Brendan McKenna been right—was she asking too much?

35

After a half-day with him, she had no doubt that the man knew his business. And yet, she just couldn't believe that the perfect house wasn't out there somewhere. Some day, and surely not too far in the future, she would walk into a house and say, this is it. This is where Graham and I will live, talk, laugh, and play, raise our children, grow old together——

She would be buying not just a house, she reflected, but a home for a lifetime, and that required a completely different sort of search.

'I won't settle for less,' she told herself. 'In a city this size, there has to be a house that is just right for us.'

The telephone on the kitchen counter rang, and she dumped Omar unceremoniously off her lap to answer it. It was Graham.

'Where have you been, Kaye? They told me at the travel agency that you'd gone to look at houses——'

'I did, Graham.' She was eager to share the results with him; her words were almost tumbling over each other. 'I haven't found anything wonderful yet, but today was just exploratory, to find out what sorts of things I like best, and——' She realised suddenly that she was babbling, and that there was no sound from the other end of the line.

'Which firm did you go to, Kaye?'

'First City.'

'But surely you know that Andy Winchester always does my buying and selling, Kaye. He's done it for years.'

Kaye had never met Andy Winchester, but she knew who he was—if there was a million-dollar building project in the wind, the Winchester firm was always involved. 'Yes,' she said. 'I knew that. But I thought he only dealt with commercial properties, banks and industries and shopping complexes——'

'Generally, he does. But as a favour to me, he has agreed to help you find our house.'

'But this agent has already spent a whole afternoon, just getting to understand what I want,' she pleaded. 'Surely——'

'Estate agents have to expect that sort of thing,' Graham said reasonably. 'They might show houses every day for a month and not sell anything at all.'

'But surely it wouldn't hurt to let him have a chance——'

'Kaye, are you involved in a charity project or are you looking for a house?'

'The house, of course. But——'

'Well, you'd be doing him a favour not to take up any more of his time,' Graham said reasonably. 'He's not likely to have anything we'd be interested in on his listings, anyway. Stop wasting his time, and let him work with people who are apt to buy from him.'

'I suppose you're right,' Kaye said unhappily.

'Of course I'm right. Andy wants to show you a house tomorrow—it sounds perfect, Kaye. It's one of the really wonderful houses in this city, done by a premier architect, and it isn't even listed for sale, because the owners don't want to have half the population of Henderson trooping through just to look at the wallpaper.'

'If it isn't for sale, Graham——'

'Oh, they want to sell it all right. Andy's a friend of theirs—that's how he knows about it. Your precious First City person could never get you in there—he's got no idea they're ready to move to Phoenix.'

She sighed. He was right, she supposed. If Brendan didn't even know that a house was for sale, how could he show it to her? A house she would have loved to own might change hands privately and she'd never even know about it. Having good connections did make a lot of difference, and Andy Winchester certainly had them.

'I wish you hadn't told Andy about us,' she said.

'What was I supposed to do? Tell him I wanted a big house so I could start a school for the disadvantaged? Come on, Kaye.'

'Of course not. But the people at that club of yours are always talking about someone, and we did agree that we wanted to keep our engagement quiet for a little while——'

'Let me assure you, my dear, that in the ten years I've known Andy, he has never breathed a word about any confidential deal, no matter how juicy the story was.'

'I'm glad to hear that. But I wish you'd warned me. It would have saved me a lot of trouble.'

'I just assumed that you would call Andy when you had time to start looking. I'm flattered, of course, but I didn't realise that you were in such a hurry,' Graham pointed out. 'And I'm sure the afternoon wasn't a total waste of time—when you see the house Andy's got in mind for us, you'll appreciate it, after looking at all those dumps today.'

She bit her lip. There was no point, she told herself, in arguing about the houses she had seen that afternoon; of course they hadn't been dumps—Brendan wouldn't have dared show her a dump—but it was a silly thing to quarrel about. If she had liked one of those houses and wanted to buy it, that would have been a different thing, of course.

'Andy knew quite a bit about this house,' Graham went on. 'I think I mentioned that the owners are friends of his, didn't I? I'll tell you all about it over dinner. Shall I pick you up in half an hour?'

'All right,' she said. I should go and get dressed, she thought. After an afternoon of houses, she felt a little grimy. And of course she wanted to go to dinner with Graham; it wasn't often that he was out of the office at this hour on a week night.

But instead of going straight to her wardrobe, she went back to the couch, where the Persian had settled down again on his cushion and was staring at her accusingly. 'Sorry, Omar,' she said. 'I didn't mean to dump you like that.'

Omar considered the matter, and then graciously forgave her and snuggled into her lap. She scratched his ears and reminded herself that Andy Winchester had known Graham for ever. They moved in the same circles, shared the same friends as well as the same clubs. Andy would know what sort of house Graham and his new bride would need, without any casting about wildly or exploring houses of all types, as she had spent the afternoon doing. That meant that dealing with Andy would be a lot easier for her in the long run, too. Besides, she told herself, what did it matter, as long as they got the right house? But she wasn't looking forward to calling Brendan McKenna tomorrow to tell him that. He had gone to a great deal of trouble today. He would probably think that she was nothing but trouble, with the dent in his car and now this, she thought gloomily.

The doorbell rang. She looked at the clock, startled. Surely she couldn't have daydreamed away a full half-hour! If Graham had arrived to pick her up and she wasn't ready——

But it had only been five minutes, which meant it couldn't be Graham. She shifted Omar up to her shoulder and went to answer the bell.

The man at the door stretched out a finger for the Persian's inspection. He was holding a white paper bag. 'Hello, Omar,' he said. 'Your house-companion forgot her sandwich—dare I call it a doggie bag, Kaye, or does he have a complex about the creatures?'

'Hello, Brendan.' She took the bag. 'Thanks for bringing it over—it was an awful lot of trouble to take for half a sandwich.'

'Oh, but it's not just any half-sandwich—it's your dinner, and I didn't want you to starve. Besides, I thought the sauerkraut had interfered with the atmosphere in my car for quite long enough. What's the matter? Something is bothering you.'

Kaye bit her lip. 'We've hit a snag, I'm afraid. Can you come in so we can talk?'

'Sure.'

'I've only got a minute,' she warned, leading him to the couch. 'Graham's picking me up for dinner, and I have to get dressed.'

'And the poor reuben sandwich will be orphaned again?' Brendan sounded quite unhappy about it. 'I've got a dinner date, too, or I'd eat it myself. After smelling it all afternoon——' He reached out to scratch the cat's chin; Omar stretched his neck out and looked blissful, and when the scratching stopped, he strolled across the couch and began stroking himself against the tweed sleeve of Brendan's sports coat. 'What's the problem?'

'I'm going to look at a house tomorrow with another estate agent.'

'Is that all? I thought Graham had come up with a creeping case of bankruptcy or something.' He didn't sound disturbed.

'You don't understand,' Kaye said, feeling a little desperate. 'Graham wants me to work with him from now on, and not with you.'

Brendan raised an eyebrow at that, but he merely looked down at the cat, who was in his lap by now, and said, 'Who is it?'

'Andy Winchester.'

He nodded. 'I see.'

'You know him, of course?'

'Everyone in town knows him. The man has quite a reputation. Well, don't worry about me, Kaye. It's all right; I hadn't spent quite all of the commission money yet, anyway——'

'Brendan, I'm really sorry——'

'And in any case, I've never even driven a BMW, so I won't mind so awfully much having to cancel my order. I hope there's still time. Don't you feel bad about it.'

She looked stricken, her green eyes huge in a white face as she stared up at him. It was just the sort of thing her father would have done, she thought—spending a windfall before he got it, because he was incapable of realising that it might not come true. Brendan McKenna would be safer playing Russian roulette, she told herself. It isn't my fault what he does, but I don't like to feel responsible. I should be glad that my association with him is over. Nevertheless—well, he had been very generous with his time, and he had seemed to be truly interested in her, not just the sale——

Stop it, Kaye, she told herself. Graham doesn't want you to deal with Brendan, and that is that.

She said, stiffly, 'I wanted to tell you myself that as of tomorrow I'll be house-hunting with Andy Winchester.'

'That's your privilege,' he said cheerfully. 'I can't say I won't mind, of course; there are limits to my self-sacrifice. But I certainly can't tell you who you should hang around with.'

'Graham has always worked with Mr Winchester.'

'And of course if he's found a person he trusts to do his buying and selling, he'd want to stay with that person. That doesn't mean you can't ever talk to me, and if I

find something I think you'd like, we can still go look
at it.'

Kaye shook her head. 'Graham doesn't want me to,'
she said. 'He thinks I'd just be wasting your time.'

Brendan's jaw tightened just a little. It made her the
slightest bit uneasy. 'It's my time to waste.'

'I think it would be best if we just forgot the whole
thing. Graham was very definite about it.'

Now there was no doubt about it; he was smouldering.
So Brendan McKenna has a temper after all, Kaye
thought. She was glad it was Graham he was angry at,
and not her.

'Tell me,' he said, very gently, 'has Graham always
shown this tendency to jealousy?'

'Of course not—jealous? What on earth do you
mean?' Then she started to laugh. 'Do you think that
Graham might actually be jealous of you? Don't be ridiculous! Graham's a businessman—he's not the sort to
let personal feelings interfere. And he doesn't even know
you, anyway.'

'You sound very certain of that,' Brendan said. 'But
of course you're correct—what on earth am I thinking
about? Graham Forrest has no reason to be jealous of
any man on earth—certainly not a mere insect like me.'

'That wasn't what I meant——' She realised, belatedly, how very tactless she must have sounded.

'Don't apologise for telling the truth,' he said, and
there was a hard edge to his voice. 'I just thought it was
possible that Graham didn't want you associating with
any males under the age of sixty. I stand corrected, and
I'm happy for you.' He rose, and Omar yowled at being
evicted from a warm lap.

Kaye jumped up too, uncertain of how to patch up
the mess she'd made.

'Thank you for telling me about this yourself, Kaye,' he said, more gently. 'It would have been much easier, I'm sure, to have said nothing at all, and just given me excuses whenever I found a house to show you.'

She followed him to the door, eager to defend herself. 'I'm not that kind, Brendan. I couldn't just let you think that I didn't even appreciate what you'd done, or that I was only having a good time at your expense this afternoon——'

He smiled then. His dark blue eyes had a fascinating glow. 'I never would have thought that, Kaye, no matter what.' He held out a hand to shake hers. 'Good luck.'

'Thanks for lunch,' she said uncertainly. Her hand slipped out of his warm grasp, and he pulled his gloves on.

'My pleasure,' he said. Then he was gone into the cold night.

Graham took her to his favourite club for dinner, where Andy Winchester joined them for dessert. Kaye tried to stifle a yawn as she ate her chocolate mousse, and found herself wondering where Brendan was having dinner, and with whom. The exotic brunette from the estate agency, perhaps? In any case, she concluded, it was a safe bet that he was having more fun than she was.

The next afternoon Kaye and Andy Winchester toured the Aynsley mansion in Henderson Heights. And that evening, in her apartment, Kaye and Graham had their first quarrel.

It was not a fight in any sense of the word; it was instead a coldly civil discussion. But it was none the less bitter, and it ended up with Kaye nearly in tears.

'I can't work with Andy Winchester,' she tried to explain to Graham. 'He wouldn't even listen to what I want—he just kept telling me what I should have.'

The problem had actually started with her first glimpse of Andy Winchester. He was over seventy, she estimated, and slightly hard of hearing. He liked to punctuate his statements with a wave of a battered old black cigar, which was foul-smelling despite the fact that it wasn't lit. Kaye was not impressed.

She was even less convinced that she should put her trust in him when the tour started. Mrs Aynsley had greeted them at the door with a cheerful smile. It was an intriguing house; it looked like a rectangular block that had been twisted by a giant and tossed aside. Graham was right about one thing; the architecture was strikingly unusual.

But within ten minutes, Kaye knew that it was also an impossible house, by her standards. The windows were huge, but Mrs Aynsley had the light shut out with heavy curtains, and when Kaye pulled one open, she discovered that the patio overlooked the golf course of one of Henderson's most exclusive clubs. It wasn't like having a public playground in the back yard, Kaye thought, but it was scarcely private, either. Anyone playing the course could look straight through the house unless the curtains were closed. What sense was there in having windows at all, she asked herself, if you couldn't let the light in and you had no idea when one of them would explode under the weight of a stray golf ball? She shook her head at Andy Winchester.

'Thank you, Mrs Aynsley,' he said, his voice booming. 'I'm sure Mr Forrest will want a day or two to think about it before he makes an offer. You're not going to hold these young people up, are you?'

Mrs Aynsley fluttered and giggled. 'Oh, Andy,' she said. 'You know we have to get a good price. And that other buyer you found—well, it was a good offer, even if it wasn't as high as we'd like.'

Kaye strode down the path to Andy Winchester's new Cadillac and slammed the door with unnecessary force. 'I don't think there is another buyer.'

'Why, there most certainly is,' he sputtered.

Kaye was not convinced. 'In that case,' she said, 'you had better advise Mrs Aynsley to take his offer, because I am not interested in buying that house at any price!'

'They're really very anxious to sell,' he said. 'I think you and Graham should make your offer right away. It's the best value on the market in this city right now, and you will never see a house like it again.'

'Frankly, Mr Winchester, if they were asking a dollar and a half for that house I wouldn't be interested.'

'Well——' For the first time, he seemed to falter a bit. 'Of course, a good decorator could do a lot with it, Kaye——'

That was the final straw. 'And I don't recall asking you to call me Kaye!'

She told Graham all about it that night, and was in tears by the time she had finished.

He seemed to think that she was being a little ridiculous. 'Honestly, darling, what does it matter what he calls you?' he said, patting the couch cushion in an invitation for her to sit beside him. Omar stared at the glitter of Graham's cuff-link, and pounced. Graham swore and pulled back, eyeing the cat malevolently. 'Andy's right about it being the best value on the market just now, you know. The Aynsleys aren't even asking the full amount that the appraiser said it was worth.'

Kaye didn't sit down; she was too agitated. 'Graham, you haven't even looked at the place. How can you be so certain you'd like it?'

'I haven't looked at it,' he said reasonably, 'because we decided that looking for a house was your job. When you've found the one you like, then I'll go and see it.'

She collapsed on to the sofa beside him, feeling suddenly exhausted. 'Well, I haven't found the one I like. I have absolutely no intention of living in the Aynsley house.'

Graham sighed. 'Very well. I'll tell Andy that we aren't interested in making an offer at this time——'

'Or at any other time, either,' Kaye said obstinately.

'Kaye, darling, do be reasonable. We're looking for a very large house, and there just are not many in town.'

'You're the one who had the long list of requirements,' she pointed out. 'I asked for a convenient place to do the laundry, and a big kitchen.' That wasn't quite accurate, but Kaye felt that she was under attack.

'And I've tried to tell you that you don't need to worry about those things. You don't think I'm going to let these handsome fingers get hurt by dishwater, do you?' He picked up her hand. 'Find yourself a pretty house, my dear, and let the maid worry about how far she has to walk with the laundry. You'll be far too busy with your friends, and with the parties, and with the children——'

She sighed. 'All right, Graham,' she said. 'I'll stop looking for the perfect house, and if I find anything reasonable, I'll consider it very carefully.'

'That's my girl.'

'But I just can't work with Andy Winchester,' she pleaded. 'I simply don't trust the man, and I don't think I can honestly evaluate anything he shows me.'

Graham looked wary. 'What are you suggesting, Kaye?'

She sighed. 'I'd like to go back to the other agent that I was working with,' she said finally. The one, she reminded herself, who is so sure he can sell me a house that he bought himself a BMW on speculation. Oh, stop it, Kaye, she thought. It's none of your business. Besides, he was probably only joking.

'Who is this upstart, anyway?'

'His name is Brendan McKenna.'

Graham shook his head. 'I've never heard of him. What do you know about him, anyway? Do you have any references? Have you talked to any satisfied clients? Do you even know how long he's been in the business?'

'No,' Kaye admitted, 'but I trust him.'

'Kaye, you're a babe in the woods. You are so innocent, my dear——' He sighed. 'All right. Have it your own way. But I'm putting some conditions on this. If he finds a house you want, I'm going to have it inspected right down to the last square inch of tile in the bathrooms.'

'Fair enough,' Kaye said.

'And I'm going to check on your Mr McKenna.'

'I don't think you'll find anything shady.'

'You'd better hope I don't. Now,' Graham said, putting his arm across the back of the couch, 'can we talk about some fun things? Like us, and where we're going on our honeymoon?'

CHAPTER FOUR

'WELL?' Emily demanded the next morning, before Kaye had even taken off her heavy coat. 'Was it the dream cottage you're looking for?'

Kaye thought about the Aynsley house and grimaced. 'It certainly wasn't.'

Marilyn came out of her office. 'Don't be discouraged, Kaye,' she recommended. 'I get the urge to go house-hunting once a year or so, and I look till I get depressed. I haven't found anything yet, and my needs aren't nearly as involved as yours.'

'I didn't know you were thinking of moving.'

Marilyn nodded. 'Our big old home is getting to be too much for me to handle——'

'Big?' Kaye asked brightly. 'Old?'

Marilyn laughed. 'Neither big enough nor old enough to suit you and Graham, I'm afraid. It's not exactly in Henderson Heights, either.'

'I looked at a house the other day that might suit you. Why don't you call Brendan about it? Or I could mention it to him—I'll be talking to him this morning.' She was looking forward to calling him. He would be so pleased—and surprised—to hear from her.

'Would you, Kaye? I like to look at houses now and then, even if I don't ever find what I want.'

'I'm sure it would be fun,' Kaye said, 'if I wasn't in such a hurry to have the whole thing settled.'

'Of course you are, dear. You certainly don't want to keep Graham waiting.'

'Are you sure it's all right with you, Marilyn? I'm taking an awful lot of time off work to go rummaging through houses——'

The customer who had just walked in came over to Kaye's desk with a smile. Angela Warren was a friend of Graham's; in fact, her husband was Graham's lawyer. Kaye saw her at the club every week or two, but they had only exchanged small talk in the ladies' lounge. 'Darling,' Mrs Warren said, reaching out both hands to clasp Kaye's. 'I was so pleased to hear the news!'

'News?' Kaye said, feeling a little blank.

'Of your engagement, of course. I heard it at the club last night, and I'm so happy for you both.'

Some secret we're keeping, Kaye thought. I knew when Graham told Andy Winchester that it would be all over town! Then she scolded herself. It might not have been Andy who had talked, after all; she certainly couldn't accuse him without proof. At any rate, the only way to handle it now was to be gracious. 'Thank you, Angela. It was very thoughtful of you to stop by.'

'Oh, I just had to come and give you my best wishes. Graham's always been one of my favourites, you know.'

'We hadn't planned to make a formal announcement right away,' Kaye warned, 'because we haven't set a wedding date.'

'I see that you aren't even wearing your ring yet. And I understand perfectly. Don't worry; I can keep it under my hat,' she added airily. 'Actually I came in for something else as well. My grandson wants to come and visit us next month. But his parents can't come along. Will any of the airlines let him fly by himself?'

'I'm sure we can make arrangements,' Kaye said, turning to her computer terminal. 'How old is he?'

She sensed, rather than saw, Marilyn's satisfied smile. Her strategy, the woman seemed to be thinking, was working; Kaye's new connections could be very profitable for Gulliver's Travel.

When she called the estate agent, Brendan answered, and the surprise in his voice when she identified herself was all she could have hoped for. 'You didn't like the house you saw yesterday?' he hazarded.

'No, and I liked the person who showed it to me even less. I told Graham I wanted to deal with you, or nobody.'

'That wasn't very wise of you.'

Kaye was silent for a long instant. 'What does that mean?' she challenged. 'Don't you want my business any more?'

'Of course I want your business. But you really shouldn't start handing down ultimatums to the man until the knot is tied. It isn't wise to make him wonder if you're really going to be the respectful little wife he thinks he's getting—you know, with the house in the suburbs, the two-point-four kids, the dog, the bridge club, and the station wagon——'

'You know, it sounds deadly dull when you put it that way.'

'Precisely,' he said cheerfully. 'Which is why you don't want Graham to start thinking about it. If he does, I won't get my BMW, and you wouldn't want that to happen, would you?'

'I thought you said you'd given up the idea.'

'Oh, I have. It would be a terribly impractical car for me, anyway—I need space when I'm driving clients around. But it's fun to think about.'

Kaye laughed at his airy tone. He was only joking, she told herself in relief. I should have known it. I'm just too sensitive to things like that! 'If it makes you feel better, I didn't really give Graham an ultimatum; I just said I'd rather work with you. Do you have anything to show me this afternoon? I'll buy lunch; it's my turn.'

'Can't. I've got plenty to show you, but I have another appointment. How about tomorrow?'

How absolutely ridiculous to feel disappointed, she told herself flatly. She certainly hadn't expected that he would hang around the office waiting to hear from her—or had she, half-consciously? She should be glad that he had other prospects.

'All right,' she said finally. 'I'll see you tomorrow, then.'

'Don't fret,' he said. 'Nothing you want is going to sell in the next twenty-four hours.'

Emily had answered the other line while Kaye was talking, and now she banged the receiver down hard. 'That is the sixteenth call this week,' she said irritably. 'One of the other agencies is pushing a tour, and everyone is confused and calling us about it.'

'What is it?' Kaye asked idly. 'It must be a good deal, to excite that much interest.'

'You don't know about it?' Then Emily answered her own question. 'Of course not. You've been out house-hunting instead of here answering the telephone.'

'Sorry, Emily. What's the tour?'

'They're taking a chartered plane to the Bahamas for one day. Can you imagine anyone flying half-way across the country for a few short hours in Nassau?'

'Yes,' Kaye said. She could almost feel the warmth of the sun on her bare back, the scrape of the sand against winter-softened toes, the kiss of the blue water against delicate skin.

'The plane takes off at some dreadful hour, just to get to the Caribbean while it's still morning, and they'll be on their way home before the sun even goes down.

But people are wild about it.' She shook her head. 'I don't understand.'

'I'd go,' Kaye said. 'Even one day in the sun, on the beach—but I don't have the money.'

'You,' Emily said tartly, 'will probably be going twice a year. You'll be able to do anything you like, while the rest of us are stuck here answering the telephone for the rest of our natural lives——' It rang imperiously, and she picked it up again.

Kaye wanted to say, It isn't going to change me, Emily——

Then she decided that silence was the wiser course, and turned back to her own work. Being engaged to Graham might not make her into a different person, but she sadly concluded that it had already altered other things. Marilyn's treatment of her had certainly changed, and so had Emily's attitude.

Emily put the telephone back in place. 'I'm sorry,' she said. 'I sound like a jealous witch, don't I? I don't mean it. I'm glad everything is going so well for you, I really am. I've just got cabin fever, I suppose.'

Kaye nodded. 'I know, Emily. It seems as if winter will never end, doesn't it?' But she didn't forget the outburst, and she didn't think that Emily did, either.

She found the house on Friday. It clung to the side of a hill in the steepest and newest section of Henderson Heights. The house was only three years old, Brendan told her, but its cedar-shingled exterior had weathered to a silvery grey that blended in with the maples and oaks that surrounded it. It really didn't look like a large house at all from the outside, but she walked from room to room with glee, counting bedrooms and imagining herself following a day's routine in these beautiful surroundings. The kitchen was smaller than she had hoped for, but the view was superb. The carpeting in some of the rooms was a peculiar shade of pale pink, but that, she told herself stoutly, could be changed in a hurry. To balance that disadvantage, though, there was a huge glassed-in porch that she knew instinctively would be her favourite room.

She stood on the balcony outside the master bedroom, staring off across the tree-lined valley. Just now it was blanketed with snow, and it was beautiful. But in summer, she thought, it would be perfect here. There would be birds to watch, and squirrels to feed, and something new to notice every day.

The house was empty, which meant they could start to work as soon as the paperwork was done, and they could set an early wedding date. Graham will be pleased about that, she thought.

The wind sweeping up through the valley was cold, but she didn't notice it until Brendan came out on to the balcony beside her. It wasn't until she felt his warmth that she started to shiver, and then she began to laugh at herself.

'And I thought I couldn't be happy with anything but an old house,' she said. 'Brendan, thank you. This is it.' She gestured toward the valley. 'It's perfect.'

'The setting is wonderful, isn't it? Of course, there are some things to be done, but with three full levels it's got space for you to work with.'

'Can I sign the papers?' she asked. 'I'd hate for someone else to come along and buy it, now that I've finally found it.'

'Don't you think Graham should see it first?'

'Oh—of course. How silly of me.' She shook her head in confusion. 'Perhaps tomorrow?' she said. 'I know it's Saturday, but it's hard for him to get away from the office during the week——'

'Fine,' Brendan said. 'I don't mind working weekends in a good cause.'

'And a new BMW would be a very good cause,' Kaye murmured innocently. 'We're going to look at rings right after lunch tomorrow—could we meet you here at the house at two?'

'That's fine with me. Now, shall we lock up and go have a drink to celebrate?'

She smiled up at him, a child's happy grin. 'Let's!'

'Where would you like to go?'

'Not anywhere close to the plaza,' Kaye said. 'I feel guilty enough about not rushing straight back to work for the rest of the afternoon.'

Brendan grinned. 'One of many advantages of property selling,' he said. 'I can set my own hours, and no one complains.'

'Including weekends and evenings,' Kaye pointed out. 'Doesn't your family mind?'

'No family. Just a neighbourhood tomcat who keeps an eye on me, and lets me know when I'm late coming home.'

She twisted around in her seat. There was no stuffed animal in the back of the car. 'I would have sworn that you were hauling a teddy bear around last time I rode with you.'

'Oh, that. It was my niece's—she left it here last weekend. I understand it caused something of a storm in Lakemont, Wisconsin when it turned up missing. I had to send it back to her by express mail.'

Kaye giggled.

'Don't laugh,' he recommended. 'You've never met a young lady as determined as my niece. So, let me get this straight—from one teddy bear, you deduced that I had a wife and a couple of kids?'

'More like half a dozen,' she said demurely. 'It was a very battered teddy bear. Not that I have anything against large families, you understand——'

'I should hope not, since you are buying a five-bedroom house.'

The reminder sobered her a bit. She had enjoyed this week, and she realised for the first time that it was really over. She had found her house, and now there would be no more adventures with Brendan.

'One thing about a house that size,' he went on. 'You won't be lacking for something to do, even without your job.'

She looked at him in astonishment. 'I'm not planning to give up my job,' she said.

'You amaze me.'

The tone of his voice was calm enough, but it aggravated her, because it seemed to be the same attitude that Emily had shown. 'I suppose you mean that because Graham has plenty of money, I'm not planning to work.'

'The thought had crossed my mind.'

'Well, the pay cheque isn't the only reason to hold a job. There's self-satisfaction, and independence, and the feeling of being a useful part of society——'

'Then, by all means,' he said mildly, 'you have my permission to continue working.'

It was so matter-of-fact that her irritation vanished like a wisp of fog, and she started to laugh. 'I must have sounded a bit radical, didn't I?'

'Rather. Do you like the travel agency so well?'

'Yes, I do. I might not always do that, but for right now, I like it.'

'Have you worked there long?'

She shook her head. 'Only for about a year. I started there as soon as I was out of college, but I did lots of other things before that.' She had lost count of her part-time jobs, as a matter of fact. It seemed she had always had a job of some sort, from babysitting the neighbours' kids to waiting at tables. There had never been enough money, and so, from the time she was old enough, Kaye had tried to help out.

He didn't ask any further questions, and something deep inside her was just a little disappointed that he didn't want to know more. That was silly, she told herself. She really knew very little about him, either, and it was only idle curiosity that made her want to know more.

As they passed the Aynsley house, she shuddered. 'And to think that Andy Winchester wanted me to buy that,' she said.

'Cliff Aynsley's house? Not your style at all, I should think. I always had the impression that the architect who designed it had been hitting the firewater a little too hard at the time.'

Kaye blinked in confusion. His tone was casual, as if he knew the house well. 'You've seen it?'

He nodded. 'We had it listed last year. We must have shown it a thousand times, but we didn't get a single offer. I thought they were trying to sell it themselves now—but you say they've listed it with Winchester?'

'It's not exactly listed.' So that was what the truth was, Kaye thought. She could hardly wait to tell Graham about this—how his favourite estate agent had been trying to sell him a turkey that no one else wanted, and not a mansion so exclusive that no one else even knew it was for sale!

Graham had been so certain that Brendan couldn't possibly know about the sort of house they would want to buy. He'd been wrong about that, too, Kaye thought triumphantly. She was looking forward to proving it to him tomorrow, when he saw their new house for the first time.

It was without a doubt the most stunningly elaborate engagement ring Kaye had ever seen. It must have cost Graham a fortune, she thought weakly as she stared down at the huge emerald winking on her finger. On each side of the big square-cut stone was a fan of baguette diamonds, and the band itself was lined with tiny emeralds, perfectly matched and cut.

It felt as if she were wearing a searchlight. But that's just because I've never had anything really glamorous before, she told herself. My jewellery has always been plain and simple, mostly because I couldn't afford anything else. It will just take me a little while to get used to having things like this.

'It's beautiful,' she told Graham. 'But I thought you said we were coming to the jewellers today just to look.'

He beamed. 'That's what I intended. But I stopped in earlier this week to let them know the sort of thing I wanted you to have, and as soon as I saw that stone, I knew it was yours. It's just the colour of your eyes, you know.'

'It's very rare,' the jeweller agreed, 'to find an emerald that size, and so perfect. Of course, we've had a bit of a rush getting it ready for you by today.'

'I designed the setting myself,' Graham said modestly. 'We had to guess at the size—is it all right?'

'It feels just a little tight.'

The jeweller nodded, but said, 'I'd recommend you try it for a day or two first. You may want a snug fit to keep it from slipping—it is quite a heavy ring.'

He could say that again, Kaye thought. She felt as if it took conscious effort to keep her left hand from dragging on the pavement as they left the shop.

'Now that's taken care of,' Graham said, with satisfaction in his voice, 'let's go and look at this house. If you're right, and it really is satisfactory, we can set a date. Tell me, Kaye, would you like to be a June bride?'

June, she thought dreamily. Warm weather and sunshine—an organza wedding gown trimmed in delicate lace—the soft scent of daisies and summer roses . . . 'I'll be glad to have a date set,' she said. 'It's a little embarrassing to keep getting congratulations from people before the announcement's even been made. Angela Warren came into the travel agency this week to wish me well, and just yesterday she asked if we'd set a date yet——' She swallowed the rest of that statement; having a drink with Brendan in the middle of the afternoon to celebrate had been above board and perfectly acceptable, but she wasn't quite sure how Graham would take it, especially if he found out that they had run into his lawyer's wife at that quiet little bar. Angela Warren had looked quite intrigued herself. It had made Kaye nervous, and she'd been a little clumsy when she introduced Brendan. Angela hadn't missed that, either, Kaye was sure.

'Has that been happening to you, too? There will be a lot of interest in us, I'm afraid. But the time will go by before we know it. You said the house was in good shape, though?'

She nodded. 'Of course there are things I'd like to change, but nothing that *has* to be done. We could actually move into it right away, if we wanted.' She couldn't resist a jab. 'Unlike the Aynsley house, which would have taken a year of work.'

She had told him over lunch what Brendan had said about the Aynsley house. Graham had shrugged off the story. Now he said calmly, 'I doubt Andy knew all the details. He was only doing it out of friendship, anyway.'

'Friendship for whom? You or the Aynsleys? It looks to me as if you would have been left holding the bag.' She leaned forward in her seat. 'Look, Graham. You can catch just a glimpse of the house there on the hillside.'

'Where? I didn't see anything.'

'That's one of the beauties of it, I think. It's so private that unless you know exactly where to look, you can't see it at all. The driveway is up the next hill and off to the right, and Brendan should already be there.'

'You're on a first-name basis?'

'Yes,' she said mildly. 'Do you object?'

'I don't suppose it makes any difference.'

'What did you find out about Brendan?' She was relatively sure of the answer, or she wouldn't have asked the question. Graham had had nearly a full week to make his enquiries, and it seemed to her that if he had found anything to discredit Brendan McKenna, he would have told her about it within the hour.

'He seems to be reputable.' It was stiff, almost grudging, and Kaye interpreted it to mean that everything Graham had heard was glowing. 'He only sells houses, though. Nobody seems to know why, but it's a little short-sighted, I'd think. The big money is in commercial property, and it's a whole lot less bother, too.' He parked beside a brand-new dark blue car in the driveway. Brendan's car was nowhere to be seen.

Kaye glanced at her watch in irritation. This is no time to be late, McKenna, she thought.

But Brendan greeted them at the door. 'Hello, Kaye. Mr Forrest——' His hand was extended.

Graham shook hands politely and turned to his left, into the formal living-room. He stood in the centre of the room for a moment.

'I didn't think you were here yet,' Kaye said. 'Your car isn't——' Suspicion edged into her voice.

'Do you like it?' Brendan asked.

'You borrowed it while yours is being fixed, right?'

He shook his head. 'No. I decided I'd had the old one long enough, so I rewarded myself.'

'You told me you'd given up the idea.' She was furious.

'Of a BMW, yes. I never said I wasn't going to buy a car, Kaye, and why you think it's any of your business——'

'You idiot,' she said, and her voice was taut with anger. 'You're a damned fool, Brendan McKenna——'

He looked stunned, as if she had slapped him, and Kaye stopped short, her face burning. Just why did she think it was any of her affair? Besides, she told herself harshly, he hadn't done anything so very irresponsible. She and Graham were going to buy the house, weren't they? He'd get the commission; there was no doubt about that. And you, she lectured herself, have no business to be telling him what to do with his money——

She turned on her heel, followed Graham into the living-room, and slipped a trembling hand through his arm to steady herself.

Brendan paused in the doorway for an instant, a frown of puzzlement creasing his forehead as he watched the couple across the room. Then, with a long breath that sounded almost like a weary sigh, he followed them. His shoulders seemed to sag a little.

Graham paced thoughtfully down the length of the room, up a step and into the attached dining-area, which was set off from the living-room with a wrought-iron railing. His eyes were on the carpet.

'That dreadful pink has to go, of course,' Kaye said. Her voice wasn't quite steady, but she had command of herself again. She let go of his arm and turned around to look across the room with half-closed eyes. 'I think something in off-white or light grey would be much more versatile——'

'Hmmm,' Graham said. He vanished through the door that led to the kitchen.

For an instant, Kaye was almost afraid. Now that they were alone again, what would Brendan say? Would he demand an explanation of the harsh accusation she had flung at him? He certainly had every right to.

But he didn't. Instead, he murmured, 'I see the jeweller had your kind of glitter in stock, after all. I thought perhaps your ring would have to be specially ordered.'

'It was,' Kaye said. 'Graham designed it.'

He studied her face for a long moment. Then he took hold of her hand and his eyes dropped to the ring. 'How very interesting.' There was no expression in his voice.

Kaye flushed in embarrassment, and then was heartily ashamed of herself. What difference did it make what Brendan McKenna thought of her engagement ring, anyway? Graham had spent his precious time designing a ring, when most men would have settled for the first ordinary diamond that they saw. How dared Brendan sneer at it! She glanced down at her hand and sighed wistfully.

'I think that sigh must mean that he designed it without even asking what you wanted,' Brendan hazarded.

'And I think that it's a beautiful ring and—and none of your business.'

He let her fingers slip out of his, and the weight of the ring dragged her hand down. 'That's true,' he said. 'It certainly is none of my affair. Shall we catch up with your multi-talented fiancé?'

Graham was upstairs by then, inspecting the master bedroom.

Brendan waved a hand at the bedroom across the hall and said, 'I think you'll find this to be quite a comfortable house for a family, Mr Forrest. The nursery is just across the hall and the entertainment centre downstairs would make a wonderful playroom. It would be very easy to keep track of the children.'

Graham looked at him with disbelief and said, 'That's only another way of saying that they'd always be underfoot!'

It didn't disturb Brendan. 'Nothing of the sort,' he said. 'As soon as they are old enough, they can be moved down to the bedrooms on the lower level. The entertainment centre could be sound-proofed so if you wanted to have a party, it wouldn't disturb the children.' He was smiling calmly.

Graham didn't bother to answer that one. 'Kaye,' he said, 'now that you've had your little joke, shall we get down to some serious house-hunting?'

'I don't understand,' she said. 'I am serious, Graham——'

Graham waved a hand. 'This is absolutely impossible, Kaye. There isn't even space for a maid's room.'

'The maid is going to live with us?' she asked weakly.

'The dining-room will only seat six, at best. The entire house is far too small to entertain properly——'

'But you haven't even looked at the lower level. There is an enormous room down there——'

'Are you really suggesting that I entertain my clients and my friends in a basement, Kaye? How do you plan to give dinner parties—by setting up a buffet on a ping-pong table? I think you must have gone completely mad.' He glanced at Brendan. 'Or else you have fallen into the clutches of an unscrupulous salesman.'

'That's ridiculous, Graham! Brendan is not unscrupulous——' She was almost in tears.

'Certainly not unscrupulous,' Brendan said calmly. 'But perhaps confused. If we could sit down and talk about what you'd like to have, Mr Forrest——?' He indicated a window-seat.

'I thought I had made things clear to Kaye,' Graham said, but he settled himself on the seat.

'Yes, I believe Kaye thought you had, too. It happens sometimes; a client falls in love with a house and is completely blind to its faults. Now, if we can just talk it over——'

Kaye was furious. Isn't that just like two men? she thought. When something goes wrong, they blame the woman!—and then they go off and discuss it without even including her. Dammit, this is going to be my house! Shouldn't I at least have a say in it?

But they had their heads together, and they obviously weren't going to listen to anything she said.

She retreated to the first floor, her resentment building into a storm. If there had been a china vase handy, she would have smashed it.

So she had fallen in love with the house, had she? And she had become completely blind to its faults! At least now she knew where she stood with Brendan McKenna, she thought resentfully—precisely nowhere! He hadn't even backed her up; as soon as he saw which way the wind was blowing, he had promptly deserted her cause and agreed with Graham. Well, that shouldn't have surprised her, she decided. She certainly didn't have the money to buy a house; it was Graham's funds that would, in the long run, pay for Brendan's commission.

And that, she thought spitefully, was what he was counting on to pay for that spanking new car. She should have expected that he'd abandon her as soon as his commission was threatened! Well, I hope he has to eat the damned car, she thought vindictively.

When Graham and Brendan came downstairs twenty minutes later, apparently the best of buddies, she looked at them both with silently smouldering anger.

'Well,' Brendan said cheerfully, 'I'll get to work, and next week we'll have some new things to look at, Kaye.'

'Don't bet on it,' she muttered, and swept out to Graham's car with an icily regal air that the best royal families would have envied.

CHAPTER FIVE

KAYE maintained an obstinate silence half-way across town, and then realised that giving Graham the silent treatment was going to accomplish less than nothing. So she finally cleared her throat, gathered her poise, and said, 'I like that house, Graham.'

Amazingly enough, he didn't argue. 'It is a very nice house, darling. But it is simply not suited for us. I can't imagine how you allowed yourself to be so short-sighted about it; even your estate agent was pointing out flaws that I'll bet you had never seen.'

'I didn't hear him pointing out any flaws,' she muttered. There must have been quite a heart-to-heart discussion going on between the two of them, she thought, while she had been downstairs steaming with anger.

'You must not have been really listening. That probably accounts for the whole misunderstanding. Come, Kaye, you don't expect that he's going to walk from room to room telling you in plain English what's wrong. You have to learn to listen to what he means—not just the words he's saying.'

'I thought he was saying it was a wonderful house!'

'You obviously aren't sensitive to the implications, Kaye. Though, as a matter of fact, I can't blame you too much. I hardly believed myself that he was saying those things—I can't imagine how he ever sells a house if he keeps telling the buyers everything that's wrong with the place.'

'Unlike Andy Winchester,' Kaye murmured sweetly.

Graham nodded. 'That's right,' he said, very seriously, and Kaye longed to throw something at him. So much for being sensitive to implications, she thought viciously. Sometimes Graham himself was downright dense!

'Or perhaps he actually didn't realise that those things were flaws,' Graham went on, as if he was talking to himself. 'I can't think how McKenna got the reputation he has, if he can't read a client any better than that.'

He walked her to the door of her apartment and left her with a reminder that he'd be back at six to pick her up for the evening. 'I hope you'll find a smile by then,' Graham said. He turned her face up to his and put a quick kiss on her cheek. 'It will do no good to pout, Kaye. You're simply going to have to accept the fact that you can't always have everything you want.'

Then he was gone, leaving her standing on the step with her mouth open. It took a moment for his meaning to sink in, and then fury rose like a geyser from deep inside her. The idea, she stormed, of him implying that she was nothing more than a spoiled baby, throwing a temper tantrum because she couldn't have the house she wanted!

She slammed the apartment door behind her and smiled grimly as the whole building seemed to shake under the impact. 'Oh, I always get what I want,' she said sarcastically. 'That's why I'm living in a one-room apartment on Williams Street—because I really couldn't stand one of those elegant new condos downtown!'

Omar looked at her warily from the opposite end of the couch, decided she was not approachable, and put one paw over his eyes as if he couldn't bear the sight.

The doorbell rang. It made her feel a little happier, since Graham had apparently thought better of that last careless remark and had come back to apologise.

Then she saw who was standing on her doorstep. 'The word on the doormat does not apply to you,' she said icily. 'You are not welcome. You are a traitor, and I want nothing further to do with you.' She would have closed the door, but there was a large foot in a very nice black wingtip shoe blocking the way. Damn, she thought. I don't know exactly what he wants, but if I let him in, I'll probably never get rid of him.

Brendan said, mildly, 'A traitor? I merely recognised the realities of the situation, and dealt with them appropriately.'

'Just what is that supposed to mean?'

'Graham is never going to buy that house, Kaye. You know it, even if you won't admit it, and I know it. If we had both stayed adamant about it, we wouldn't have changed his mind, but we would have convinced him that we'd both gone completely berserk. He would have told you to have nothing more to do with me——'

'At the moment,' Kaye said bitterly, 'I can't think that it would be any great loss.'

Brendan ignored the interruption. '—and you would have had to go back to looking at houses with Andy Winchester.'

'You really know how to hurt a girl's feelings, McKenna.'

'It's true, whether you like it or not. May I come in?'

'No. You're just coming back because you need the commission to pay for that new car!'

'What difference does it make to you how I spend my money?' he asked quietly.

'Because it isn't your money yet!'

'I'm not embezzling it, Kaye.' He shook his head sadly. 'You shouldn't be so angry at me. In fact, you should be grateful that I kept my head.'

'I thought you were trying to *sell* houses, not talk people out of buying them!'

'I had no reason to suspect Graham might veto it. After all, you did tell me he said you could choose your own house.'

'He did.'

'Well, obviously, he didn't mean it. It didn't take long to see the way things really work with Graham Forrest.'

She resented the fact that he'd dared to say that, but she had to admit he was partly right. Graham had told her she could choose her house freely, and she could—as long as it met every one of his requirements.

'Instead of adding to the calamity,' Brendan said reasonably, 'I pulled your chestnuts out of the fire, convinced Graham that I do know what I'm talking about and that I can restrain you from falling blindly in love with any more inappropriate houses——'

'I did not fall blindly in——' she began resentfully.

'Yes, you did. You didn't even notice that the microwave oven they'd built into that brick wall in the kitchen was too high for you to reach.'

She thought about it, and concluded with regret that he was right. 'You could have told me that yesterday,' she said, 'before I made a fool of myself.'

'Would you have cared yesterday?' It was quiet.

Yesterday, the magical spell of that wild valley had been still tugging at her. She shook her head.

'Kaye,' he said, very seriously, 'I don't gain if the buyers aren't pleased. If they don't like my work, they don't send their friends to me. I don't think you would have been happy in that house. You would have cursed me every time you tried to walk around that kitchen.'

'If you're so sure it's the wrong house for me,' she said sadly, 'then why did you even show it to me?' She was leaning against the door jamb, her face turned up to his.

There was a long pause. His eyes had turned an even darker blue, she noticed idly, and his hair was ruffled from the winter's wind. 'Because I didn't know it wasn't right till I saw you there,' he said, very quietly. 'And I had no idea you'd fall so deeply in love with it.'

'That's the house I want,' she said stubbornly. Then she added, more quietly, 'You think I'm being unreasonable, don't you?'

'Not unreasonable, exactly, but short-sighted. Graham will never consider that house, and you'll get nowhere if you insist. The situation calls for some psychology— Kaye, if you're not going to let me come in, would you at least stop leaning on the door? You're cutting off the circulation to my toes.'

'Then take your foot out of the way,' she said. 'If you think I'm going to invite you in for a glass of wine and a cosy chat, you're wrong.'

'I couldn't stay to drink it, anyway,' he said. 'I have a date tonight.'

'Well, so do I.' Then she spoiled her unconcerned pose by asking, 'Are you taking a lady out to dinner?'

He grinned suddenly, and it was like sunrise breaking over the lake. 'I might. Who knows where we'll end up? But I'm taking her to church first.'

'What a novel idea,' Kaye said drily. 'I'll bet you have a great success rate with that approach.'

'It's not bad.'

He looked very contented, and Kaye decided that there was no point in continuing that conversation; discussing his standard lines was obviously not going to disturb him. 'Psychology,' she mused. 'I'm not sure what you have in mind, but I know that I can't afford to keep taking every afternoon off work while I look. House-hunting is getting to be an expensive hobby. What do you suggest?'

'I'm not quite sure. Why don't we both sleep on it, and talk about it tomorrow? We can set up our strategy over Sunday brunch. My place, ten o'clock. I'll make waffles.'

'But——'

'The alternative,' he reminded, 'is Andy Winchester.' He slid a card into her hand and removed his foot from the door so abruptly that her weight had pushed the panel shut before she even realised that he had moved.

She glanced at the address he'd scribbled on the back of his business card, and sighed. With Andy Winchester as an alternative, what real choice did she have?

'Psychology,' she muttered as she turned back into her apartment. 'Why do I feel as if I've just been on the receiving end of a whole load of it?'

When she reached his apartment the next morning at two minutes to ten, there was no sign of life, and his car was nowhere to be seen. She checked his card; the number agreed with that on the porch post of the big, square, white-frame house. It wasn't the kind of place where she had expected him to live; though it was on the fringes of a neighbourhood of historic homes, this house had nothing particularly significant about it. It was simply one of the thousands of plain-styled square houses that had lined the middle-class streets of Henderson at the turn of the century, and which had now been divided into apartments. And there was no reason on earth, she told herself, why Brendan McKenna shouldn't live there. Certainly the fact that she was disappointed wouldn't weigh heavily with him.

And she shouldn't be particularly surprised, either, she reflected. The rents in this district were low, and the man did have a brand-new car to pay for now.

She climbed the steps. She felt a little uneasy, as if she was being watched, and she almost laughed in relief when she saw a huge orange tomcat sitting silently in the shadow of the porch railing. 'Were you what was making me feel creepy?' she asked. The cat watched thoughtfully as she rang the bell, and then he stood up, stretched, and came across to stand beside the door.

Nothing seemed to be stirring inside. Kaye snuggled her chin into the furry collar of her white rabbit-skin coat and thought about what she should do now. She wondered for a moment if Brendan's date the night before might have been more successful than he had anticipated. If so, the man might not even have come home yet.

The door swung silently wide, and the cat slid sinuously past Brendan's feet and inside.

It was the first time she had seen him wearing casual clothes instead of a jacket and tie, and his intricately patterned dark blue wool sweater made his eyes look like reflecting pools. The sleeves were pushed up to show well-muscled forearms. His hair was just rumpled enough to make her want to comb it with her fingers, and she realised that she had never once seen him with every hair in place. This man is really dangerously good-looking, she thought, and if the woman he was with last night only wants to take him to church, she needs her head examined.

But that, she reflected, is her problem, and not mine. 'You have a visitor,' she said.

Brendan grinned. 'I know,' he said. 'And she looks wonderful in white fur, too.'

'Not me, silly. The cat. Didn't you see him sneak in? Or is he yours?'

'That's only Sultan. No one owns him; it's more a matter of him owning the neighbourhood. He's been out all night with his harem, no doubt. Come in, it's freezing.' He held the door wide.

She didn't quite know what to expect—bare rooms? orange crates? stainless steel and glass?—but as soon as she stepped into his living-room she relaxed. Of course, she thought. He had mentioned once that he was prejudiced about Victorian houses—that was why she had been disappointed that he didn't live in one. Nevertheless, he had surrounded himself with bits of the elegance of that bygone era. 'That's a beautiful Eastlake table,' she said, running a gentle hand over its glossy marble top. 'I've got one almost like it.'

'I know. I spotted it the first time I was in your apartment.'

'It was my grandmother's—the only thing I have of hers.' Kaye's voice was wistful. 'If my father had ever found out what it was worth, he'd have sold that, too.'

'You're lucky, at that,' Brendan said. 'I've had to collect mine at auctions, because my mother is still using all the family stuff.'

'I'm surprised you live here. I don't know what I expected—a Victorian, perhaps, or something thoroughly modern.'

'I move around.'

She shivered at the memories that stirred in her at the casualness of his tone. Just so had her father spoken of each new move, each new rainbow. Everything would be better this time, he seemed to be saying. Only somehow, it always got worse instead.

Brendan was looking at her oddly, she realised. But he only said, 'Make yourself at home—I'll go start the waffles.'

His apartment took up most of the first floor. She wandered around the living-room, reading the titles on his bookshelves and touching the fine wood furniture with sensual pleasure. The place was so sparsely furnished that he might have just been moving in, but the antique pieces were beautiful ones.

She followed a heavenly aroma to the kitchen just as he put two plates, each bearing a perfect golden waffle, on the breakfast bar. In the corner, the orange cat was giving himself a bath beside a recently emptied food dish.

Brendan pulled out a high-backed wicker chair for her. 'Since I don't know what you like on your waffles,' he said, 'we have a little of everything—butter and maple syrup, cream cheese, marmalade, strawberries, whipped cream——'

'Everything looks wonderful,' Kaye said. 'I shouldn't, of course—the calorie level must be incredible.'

'If there is anything I detest,' Brendan said flatly, 'it is a woman who fishes for compliments by complaining about a non-existent weight problem.' He filled her coffee-cup and sat down beside her.

Kaye was incensed. 'I am not fishing for compliments!'

'Yes, you are, and you're not getting any from me. You know you look great just the way you are.'

No compliments, hmm, she thought, and smiled. Not that it mattered what he thought of her. Still, it was nice to be appreciated.

'Try the maple syrup,' he went on. 'It's the best there is. My mother smuggles it across the state line whenever she comes to visit.'

'I didn't know there were any restrictions on bringing food into Illinois.' The waffle was crisp and sizzling hot and delicious, and she was hungry.

'There aren't, but she persists in thinking it's a foreign country. She's a poet, and the people who love her have learned that it doesn't pay to make a fuss when she's a little vague on things like geography. She's also convinced that her favourite son is going to starve down here.'

'"Down here?" Where does she live?'

'Wisconsin. She's forgotten that she taught me to cook, and I don't disillusion her; I like getting care packages.'

'She sounds wonderful,' Kaye mused. Her heart twisted just a little at the idea; no one ever fixed care packages for her, or wondered if she was getting the right things to eat.

'Oh, she is. Would you like another waffle?'

'Yes, please.'

'Very good,' he applauded. 'Not a bit of hesitation.'

'You're corrupting me. How do you think we should handle Graham?'

Brendan shook his head. 'Food first, serious discussions later. How was your date last night?'

She watched as he poured waffle batter on to the griddle. It was apparent that he knew his way around a kitchen, she thought. She had been tempted last night when he started to talk about microwave ovens to ask what on earth he thought he knew about them—but now she was glad that she hadn't made a fool of herself. His kitchen was tiny and compact, but it was obviously used.

'Your mother was a good teacher,' she said.

'It's all in the wrist.' He spun the golden waffle on to her plate. His fingers were long and brown. They were poet's hands, she thought, and she wondered if he looked like his mother.

'It must have been an evening to remember,' he speculated.

'What?'

'Your date last night. You went off into a funk and forgot that you hadn't answered my question.'

'It really wasn't much. Graham was entertaining the president of one of the big supermarket chains.'

Brendan nodded understanding. 'They must buy a lot of baby food.'

'Tons and tons of it. The supermarket mogul was all right, except that he kept making suggestive statements and then winking at me. His wife was a lady—I felt sorry for her.'

'Where did you have dinner?'

'Pompagno's. I wish we'd gone to one of Graham's clubs, instead—it would have been quieter.'

'Just think.' Brendan put a fresh waffle on his plate. 'As soon as we find you a house, you can entertain Graham's buddies every evening, with all the privacy anyone could desire.'

'They're not his buddies, you know. I don't expect to find many kindred souls among Graham's business contacts.'

Brendan shrugged. 'That's life in the upper crust,' he said, with a notable lack of sympathy. 'It all balances out in the end, I expect.'

Enough of that, Kaye thought. 'How was your date? Did you and the lady have fun at church?'

'Oh, yes,' he said airily. 'I took your advice, by the way, and asked her out to dinner afterwards. Not that it did me any good—I was home in bed by midnight. Alone.'

Kaye devoured a strawberry. 'Where did you take her? The Wolfpack?'

'What's wrong with the Wolfpack?'

'Nothing. It's just not very romantic.'

'Did Graham have any better results last night than I did?'

Kaye was incensed. 'If you mean did he stay overnight, no!'

His eyes started to sparkle dangerously, and she bit her tongue. 'Then I saved a lot of money by not taking her to Pompagno's,' he said gently.

She didn't speak to him for a full minute after that. He just grinned at her and ate his waffle.

I don't have to explain anything to him, she told herself sternly. It's certainly none of his business whether I'm sleeping with Graham or not. 'Tell me about the rest of your family,' she said finally. That should be a safe enough subject, she thought.

Brendan shrugged. 'My father teaches mathematics at the university in Lakemont. I have three brothers and a sister——'

'Goodness,' Kaye said.

'It certainly wasn't my idea, but I got used to it. I remember that the four of us were disappointed when Anne came along—she's the youngest, and we wanted another boy to complete our basketball team. She didn't think much of the idea of four older brothers, either. I can't think why.'

'I would have given anything for one brother, older or younger,' Kaye mused. 'Or a sister. You have no idea how much an only child misses.'

'No wonder you want five bedrooms,' he teased. 'Have you always lived here?'

'No,' she said. 'I figured out once that I moved thirty-two times as a teenager. Before that, I can't remember how many places we lived.'

'You said you lived with your father?'

Suddenly, she wanted to tell him about it. 'Daddy was an entrepreneur,' she said, 'which is a polite way of saying that he didn't hold a regular job. He always had a new project, you see, and if he could only get the right backing to carry it out, we'd be millionaires. Of course, when it didn't work, we moved on—usually late at night, so the landlord couldn't talk to us about the unpaid rent——'

There was a long silence. She bit her lip, feeling like an idiot for sharing this hidden side of her with a man like Brendan. She'd never even told Graham about her father.

'It wasn't much of a childhood,' he said. His voice was so gentle that she wanted to drown in it. There was no condemnation, no drawing back, just tenderness.

She swallowed a half-hysterical sob. 'I used to pretend that we really lived in a big house somewhere and that we were just travelling from place to place in sort of a royal progress. I used to daydream that it was all just an adventure, and that some day we'd go back to our real home.'

He twisted a blonde curl around his finger. 'I should have thought, in that case, that being a travel agent would be the last thing you'd want to do.'

She thought about it. 'It does sound odd, doesn't it? And yet, it's always been part of my fantasies—to see Paris, and go to India, and walk along the streets of Hong Kong——'

'So where have you been so far?'

'Practically nowhere.'

He raised a questioning eyebrow. 'But there will never be a better chance——'

'Even with a discount, travelling takes money. I'm building up a nest egg at the moment.'

'For what?'

'I don't plan to ever be penniless.' She didn't realise how defensive she sounded until the words were out.

'Now I understand why Graham is so attractive to you.'

She searched his words for sarcasm and was faintly surprised when she didn't find any. But she refused to apologise for her way of thinking. 'I have to admit it will be nice to have jam with my bread and butter, for a change.' She looked at him with a challenge in her eyes.

'And he can afford a lot of jam.'

'Yes,' she said, 'he can.' There was a long silence. She had the feeling that she should explain it somehow, that it was important for him to really understand her point of view. She toyed with a spoon as she tried to put her thoughts together.

'Everyone disapproves when two people who have no common interests get married,' she said slowly. 'They think it's foolish. Yet people think it's awful when financial considerations come into it at all. Well, money worries break up a lot more marriages than hobbies do, that's certain. Does a woman love any less when she marries with her eyes open—when she chooses a man who shares her attitudes about money?'

'Not necessarily,' Brendan said coolly.

'That's right. But people insist on thinking that only those couples who fall head over heels and don't even look at consequences can possibly be truly in love. Why do people get so excited about romance, anyway?'

'Would you stop taking out your irritation on the whipped cream, Kaye? It's beginning to look like cottage cheese.'

She put the spoon down. 'People wouldn't think it was very funny if a girl started down a mountain wearing a blindfold along with her skis. And yet, when she marries a man without a dollar to his name they say, "Isn't that romantic? They're so much in love!" Well, romance doesn't last very long when the bills don't get paid, and there are a lot more important things in a marriage than love.'

'Name two.' There was a cold edge to Brendan's voice.

'Respect,' Kaye retorted. 'And a feeling of security. And shared goals. That's three, so there. Are you satisfied?'

He was staring at her with disbelief. Finally, he said, very quietly, 'Are you trying to convince me or yourself, Kaye?'

What difference does it make what he thinks of me? she asked herself wearily. I'll probably never see him again, once I have my house. It can't matter whether he has a good opinion of me or not; I know I'm not marrying Graham for his money.

But it still made her sad to think that she hadn't been able to explain exactly what she meant. She played with her fork, drawing patterns in the leftover maple syrup on her plate, and wished that he could understand.

It was Brendan who broke the silence eventually. 'Would you like another waffle?'

She considered. It sounded to her like a peace offering, and in any case, the things were wonderful. She yielded to temptation. 'Yes, I would. You could make your fortune in waffles, you know, Brendan.'

'Be the waffle tycoon of middle America? I might, if the estate agent business ever palls.'

'Why do you sell houses, anyway? Graham says the real money is in commercial property.'

'Somehow, I would expect Graham to see it that way.' His eyebrows had drawn together, and he looked angry. Kaye was startled. 'I sell houses because I like working with people. Corporations don't have much heart, and while I suppose there's a certain satisfaction in selling a piece of property to build a warehouse or a factory or a shopping mall on, it can't compare with the exhilaration of helping a young couple find their first real home.'

'I see what you mean,' she said uncertainly, 'but——'

'Dammit, Kaye, money isn't everything. I set my own schedule and I live the way I want to. I don't have to please anyone but my client and myself. If I want to spend a week on Lake Henderson in a fishing-boat, I do it. I refuse to be a slave to a time clock, or an employer, or even my own bank balance.'

'But surely you'd like to make some investments—you could have some security——'

'Certainly I keep an eye on the future,' he said. 'But I speculate for fun, not for profit. Don't you see, Kaye? I don't have to break my neck getting rich to consider myself a man. And I don't have to convince the world of anything by displaying my material possessions.'

'I suppose that nasty crack is aimed at me for wanting a big house.'

'It didn't happen to be.'

'I want security, Brendan, don't you see that? It isn't to show the world how well off I am, but for myself. I want a home I can count on——'

'Kaye, home isn't a place—it's the people who live there. You can't buy a home, no matter how much money you have.'

'As long as we're talking about buying things,' she snapped, 'that's a fancy car you're driving.'

'I'm not opposed to material possessions. There are lots of things I'd like to have. But I'm not going to give up a way of life I enjoy and work every minute of the week instead, just so I can afford to buy those things. I enjoy what I have *now*—I don't wait for the future.'

'You sound like my father.' Her voice was tremulous. She couldn't imagine herself with such an unconcerned attitude. 'What if you don't have anything in the future, Brendan?'

'Then I'll still have a lot of terrific memories. And do you know something, Kaye? They can take cars and pieces of art and antique furniture and houses away from you in bankruptcy court. But they can't take your memories. Sometimes memories are the only things that last. And I'm going to have some good ones.'

There were tears in her eyes. She wasn't quite sure why, but she knew she didn't want him to see them. 'I think my waffle's burning,' she said. He swore and turned around to tend to it, and she furtively dashed the tears away.

'It's just right.' He put the waffle on her plate.

'It scares me when you talk like that,' she said. 'You can't pay your bills with memories.'

'No. But they can keep you warm at night.' He looked down at her with a smile and ruffled her hair. 'Don't start worrying about me, love,' he said softly. 'I'll always have prospects. You said yourself I could make a fortune in waffles. The one I'm concerned about is Graham.'

'Graham?' she scoffed. She fumbled for a tissue and blew her nose. Silly, she told herself, to get all choked up about Brendan McKenna's attitude towards money! And the very idea that he could talk about Graham in that pitying tone!

'Yes,' he said. 'Tell me, Kaye—if Graham Forrest would happen to gamble once too often, and lose that business of his, what is he going to cling to? His memories of dinner with the supermarket mogul?'

CHAPTER SIX

TOGETHER, they looked at twenty houses that week. Each night, as soon as Kaye got off work, they started out on a new tour, and each night she came back to the plaza discouraged. It seemed sometimes as if she would never find what she was looking for.

They looked at a modern house that had a huge family-room with a thirty-foot ceiling, but bedrooms that were scarcely big enough for a baby's crib. She walked through that one in a hurry, and had to wait for Brendan to catch up. 'Are you still following me around to gauge how much I like a house?' she asked impatiently.

'Oh, no,' Brendan said airily. 'Not any more. Now I follow you because I like to watch how you walk.'

You asked for that one, she told herself.

They looked at a delightful Spanish stucco with a basement so wet that it could have passed for a wading pool. They looked at a nice old brick that had been re-modelled by someone who had no taste at all——

'It was re-muddled, actually,' Brendan said as he locked the door when they left.

'And the person who did it should be shot. What's next?'

They looked at a house which sprawled in a square around a central court, with an entire wing devoted to the master bedroom suite and a second, distant wing which contained the other bedrooms.

'I think Graham would like it,' Brendan told her. 'It certainly has that feeling of privacy he seems to want.

One thing about it, the kids won't disturb your sleep——'

She gritted her teeth. 'If the children need my attention, I want them to be able to disturb my sleep,' she pointed out. 'Which they can't do if they're sleeping in Cleveland, which is about how far away that wing is.'

Brendan shrugged. 'I just thought he might——'

'We are not showing Graham another house until we have the perfect one,' Kaye announced with icy determination.

'Of course not. We couldn't upset his regular schedule for minor matters. His time is too valuable.'

'If you're trying to be sarcastic, McKenna——'

'Haven't you noticed how rigid your precious Graham is? That won't change after you're married, you know. I bet he'll even make appointments for you in his pocket calendar—*Tuesday, 11 p.m., make love to Kaye*——'

'That', she said coldly, 'was uncalled for.'

'I imagine he thinks people should only make love in the dark, too.'

She bit her lip and said, 'You imagine a lot of things, Brendan. You really must get over this, you know. It's not fair of you to take your frustrations out on Graham, especially when he isn't here to defend himself.'

'It seems to me you're doing quite an adequate job of defending him,' Brendan said mildly.

'And I don't know where you got the idea that Graham doesn't want anything to do with kids.'

'Because he obviously thinks they should be seen and not heard. Graham's idea of the perfect baby is the one on the Forrest cereal box—quiet and always smiling.'

She didn't bother to answer that one.

Every day, when Kaye went to work, Emily asked about the progress they were making. Clearly she thought the whole process was crazy. 'You're spending more time with your estate agent than you are with your fiancé,' she said one afternoon.

'Graham's been very busy,' Kaye told her. 'He's got a meeting this week of all his top aides. They've come in from across the country, and it would be foolish for him not to spend as much time with them as he can.'

'But houses every night? Are you sure you're not looking at the same ones the second time around by now? I didn't think there were so many houses for sale in this city.'

'Believe me, Emily, I know what I'm doing. And I'm in a hurry to find a house, so that when Graham is free, we can make a decision and get things in motion.' She sounded airy and certain of herself, but inside she was hoping desperately that her faith in Brendan would prove to be well-founded.

One night she was held up by a late customer, and Brendan came into the travel agency to wait for her. After that, Emily really started shaking her head at Kaye's schedule. 'I know Marilyn said he was attractive,' Emily said, 'but no man as good-looking as that should be left to roam the world loose.'

'I am looking at houses,' Kaye told her, 'not at the man who's showing them to me.'

'More fool you,' Emily said.

'Emily, I am engaged.'

'That doesn't mean you're blind. And you must admit that Brendan McKenna is a handsome devil.' The next time he came in, Emily told him that he looked exactly like her second husband.

'Don't fall for that old line,' Kaye warned him. 'She's only been married once.' She turned to Emily. 'And Brendan has a steady girl—he takes her to church every week. So you're wasting your time.'

'Just my luck,' Emily groaned.

After they left the agency, Brendan said, 'How do you know I take her to church every week?'

'Instinct,' Kaye said. 'It's not doing you much good, though. Most of the time you look as though your halo is slightly askew.'

That was the night that he showed Kaye an imitation Roman villa with a fountain in the greenhouse and a mother-in-law's apartment over the garage. 'You could turn the apartment into a dormitory for the kids,' he suggested.

'We aren't going to have that many, thank you.'

'Oh? I thought Graham was determined to start a new product-testing division under his own roof——'

'You don't like him, do you?'

'It isn't a matter of not liking him,' he protested. 'It's just that I thought you were hard to please, until I met him.'

'The challenge is good for you. I'll bet you've worked more hours this week than you did all of last month.'

'And see where it's got me?' Brendan protested wearily. 'I can't sleep at night for nightmares about houses, and I haven't caught sight of a dime's worth of commissions yet.'

That was the precise moment when the frustration level got to be more than Kaye could deal with. She was standing on the fake marble floor of the greenhouse, beside the fake marble statue of a well-endowed and naked nymph who perpetually poured water into the fountain, when she started to cry.

'Hey,' Brendan said, startled. 'What's causing this?'

'I can't sleep either,' she sobbed. 'I'm so tired of houses. I look and I look, and there's nothing big enough or grand enough or good enough, and I just want to crawl home to my own four walls and my cat and never see another *For Sale* sign again——'

He put his arms around her and she cried out her frustration against the lapel of his tweed jacket while he gently rubbed her shoulder-blades. There was comfort in his arms, and she cried for a little longer than she would have if she had been alone. His shoulder was so very strong, and his fingers were so very gentle as he massaged her tense muscles, and his aftershave was so sweetly tangy to her nose. He had very nicely shaped ears, too, she noticed vaguely.

'Finished?' he asked finally.

She gave one last hiccupy sob and nodded.

'Then you'd better let go of my lapels,' he said, 'or I'm afraid I can't answer for what might happen next.'

She didn't quite know what that meant, but she released her strangle-hold on the soft tweed and stepped away. He sat down on the edge of the fake marble wall that surrounded the fountain and looked up at her thoughtfully. 'For a minute there,' he said, 'I wasn't sure whether you or the nymph were producing more gallons per minute. I think, all things considered, that we'd better give up the rest of the houses and call it a day.'

'I'm all right now,' she said doubtfully.

'And if I showed you Buckingham Palace you'd say you didn't like the wallpaper. Come on. Would you mind awfully if I run an errand before I take you back to the plaza?'

Kaye shook her head. 'No. Graham's busy with his staff meetings tonight.'

She had left work a little early that day, and the pale winter sun was just setting when he parked the car in front of a crowded little antiques shop in downtown Henderson. 'I love to rummage in places like this,' she said hopefully.

'Come on in. There's nothing clandestine about my business.' He reached into the back seat for a large cardboard box.

Kaye peered over the top. 'That's the most garish handpainted china platter I've ever seen,' she said.

He made a face at her and pulled the platter out of its newspaper wrappings.

'Did you paint it yourself, or did you buy it because you liked it? Sorry if I've hurt your feelings.'

'I have no feelings where this platter is concerned, except a deep hope that I can sell it.'

She looked at it more closely. 'It's chipped, too.'

'I know.' He held the door for her, the platter balanced casually under one arm.

'Are you trying to raise a little cash till the commissions come through?' Kaye speculated.

'If it was mine, I'd take it out to the rifle range and use it for target practice.' He put the platter down on the counter and said a cheerful hello to the man behind the counter.

'Some of Nora's stuff again?' the man asked warily, and when Brendan nodded, the shopkeeper picked the platter up and turned it over to examine the bottom for markings.

Kaye looked idly through a mug full of hat pins, but her attention was riveted on the platter. If it wasn't Brendan's, she wondered, then why on earth was he trying to convert it into cash? And who was Nora? Not the brunette at the real estate office, that was sure—he'd called her Cindy.

The shopkeeper shook his head. 'I just can't,' he said. 'Business has been bad, and I don't have a prayer of selling a piece like that. If times were better, I'd give Nora a price even if I had to keep it on a shelf in the back room, but——'

'I know, Joe. Don't fret about it. I'll think of something.' Brendan tucked the platter under his arm. 'Ready, Kaye?'

'Who's Nora?' she asked, after he had settled the platter gently into the box on the back seat, quite as carefully as if it had been Limoges. 'And why are you selling her dishes?'

'Nora is a friend of mine who has fallen on hard times.' He got into the car, but he didn't start the engine. He bit his lip and sighed. 'I suppose I'd better tell her as soon as possible.'

'There are other antiques shops,' Kaye reminded.

'I think I've tried them all this time. Joe was a last resort, and I only took it to his shop because Nora will ask about him. When she has a good piece, Joe gives her top dollar. But I hate to see him stuck with something he can't sell.'

'So you have to tell her it's worthless.'

'Something like that. Would you like to meet her? She seldom has visitors.' He didn't look at her; he was watching for a break in traffic.

'And I can help with the burden of breaking the bad news,' Kaye murmured. 'Sure, I'll be a sport. I owe you a favour.' Besides, she thought, I'm dying to meet his Nora. And, she admitted, a little surprised to be invited, as well.

'I think you'll like her. Fate has not smiled on Nora Farrell the last few years. She was only trying to make a living, and the state put her out of business.'

Kaye's eyes widened. 'What was she?' she demanded, and decided to put it delicately. 'A lady of the evening?'

Brendan laughed. 'Heavens, no! When you meet Nora, you'll be ashamed of yourself for even thinking such a thing. She was running an impromptu convalescent home—you know, taking in elderly people when they had been ill, until they were well enough to go home.'

'And the state didn't like it?'

'If you're going to charge fees for services like that, you have to be licensed,' he pointed out. 'Not that Nora was exactly getting paid, but she couldn't afford to do it free, so each person she nursed helped out with the costs——'

'It sounds to me as if the officials were splitting hairs.'

Brendan nodded. 'That's the way it seemed to me, too, but we got nowhere when we protested. We tried to tell them she was providing an important public service because most of those people couldn't afford standard convalescent care. Then we tried to explain that people weren't really paying Nora; they were just giving her a small gift of appreciation.'

'But they didn't go along with it?'

'No. Nora couldn't get licensed because there are pages of requirements, and there was nothing else she could do to earn money. Nora is seventy-three. So now she's living with her nephew and his family, and she sells a treasure now and then so she can have some of the luxuries of life—you know, frivolous things like a chocolate bar once a week and occasionally a new pair of stockings for church——'

His voice was almost fierce, and Kaye shivered.

'Sorry. I must sound as if I think it's all your fault.' He smiled crookedly at her, but there was no humour in his eyes.

'So it's Nora that you take to church every week,' she murmured. 'Your secret is out, Brendan.'

'My reputation is in your hands. I don't like to go to see her empty-handed——'

'Or, in this case, worse than empty-handed,' Kaye agreed. 'Is that why you're bringing me?'

'Would you run into the little shop on the corner and get a two-pound box of Hilliard chocolates? I'd go myself but there's no place to park. Here's the money— I'll go around the block so I don't tie up traffic.'

'Something tells me,' Kaye muttered to herself as she waited on the corner in the biting wind a couple of minutes later, the cellophane-wrapped box under her arm, hanging on to her hat in a valiant effort to keep it from going south for the rest of the winter, 'that keeping up with Brendan McKenna's Good Samaritan instincts could be a full-time job!'

The dark blue car stopped at the corner, blocking traffic, and Kaye dashed across to it. Horns were honking as she threw herself in, and her door wasn't quite shut yet when Brendan hit the gas. 'Hey,' Kaye protested. 'Are you trying out to be a stunt driver in a spy movie, or what? Here's your change. You've got expensive taste when it comes to frivolity, you know.'

'Stick the box under your coat when we go in,' he suggested. 'I used to take her Haagen-Daz ice-cream, but her nephew has two teenage boys, so Nora would get about three spoonfuls and they'd eat the rest. The chocolates she can hide in her room, if the kids don't know she's got them.'

Somehow, that was the saddest thing of all, Kaye thought—the idea that an adult woman could not have something of her own without hiding it from the people she lived with, the very ones who should be making sure that she was not wholly deprived. She swallowed hard, trying to get rid of the lump in her throat. She had the feeling that Nora Farrell would not appreciate the idea of someone crying for her.

The house they went to was a small bungalow in a middle-class neighbourhood, one of a row of identical dwellings. There was a small car in the driveway and a battered pick-up truck parked carelessly in the snow that covered the front lawn. Kaye looked at the house in horror. 'How many people live here?' she asked.

'Five.'

'Brendan, it's hardly big enough for a honeymoon cottage—'

'Certainly not by your standards,' he said.

She felt as if she'd been slapped. Was that why he had brought her, she wondered—to show her how selfish it was of her to want a big house, when other people had to live in this smashed-together fashion?

He got out of the car. 'Are you coming?'

'I don't think I need to. You've already made your point—I know that you think I'm being ridiculous about needing a big house when other people live like this——'

He looked astounded. 'I don't think any such thing.'

'But you said——'

'I meant that it is a small house, and especially after the ones we've been looking at, it seems to be about the right size for a doll. Don't take it personally.' There was an undercurrent of charm in his voice that tugged at her, pulling her away from the safe, sane shore and out into a dark, uncertain sea.

She looked up at him, and got slowly out of the car, quite as if there was an invisible string linking them together.

The teenaged boy who answered the door was wearing a ragged T-shirt with a less-than-polite phrase printed on the front of it. The television set was blaring, and the coffee-table was loaded with potato-chip bags and dirty dishes. 'Did you bring old Nora any ice-cream?' he asked by way of greeting.

'Not today,' Brendan said, with firm politeness. 'Would you tell her we're here, please?'

'Tell her yourself,' the boy suggested. His eyes were already back on the flickering TV screen.

Brendan swore under his breath and led the way down a narrow hall. When he knocked on a closed door, Kaye could hear a slight rustle inside. The door opened a bare inch, and a joyous voice said, 'Brendan! And you've brought your young lady!'

Brendan laughed and kissed the old woman's cheek. He was a first-class actor, Kaye thought; gone was the irritable and frustrated man who had obviously wanted to dust the living-room floor with that impudent teenage boy. 'Not my young lady, Nora,' he corrected. 'This is Kaye Reardon—I've told you about looking for a house for her.'

So there is a young lady, Kaye thought, if Nora knows about her. That's interesting.

'You're the one who's been keeping him so busy,' Nora said. She held out a thin, almost transparent hand to Kaye, and then the smile died suddenly out of her china-blue eyes. 'You shouldn't have brought her, Brendan,' she said in a horrified whisper. 'I can't entertain a grand lady in my bedroom——'

Kaye took the slender hand and impulsively leaned forward to kiss Nora's cheek. She smelled of lavender-scented soap, Kaye thought, and wondered if that had been another frivolity provided by Brendan. Nora was wearing a pale-blue dress with an old-fashioned cameo pinned to the tiny ruffle at the throat. She stood so straight that it seemed to Kaye that she probably never bent over at all. 'I came to see you, not the furniture,' Kaye said.

'Oh,' Nora said. 'You were right, Brendan. She is a lady.'

'Of course she is,' he said, in a teasing half-whisper. 'I wouldn't inflict anyone on you who wasn't. She's also carrying contraband.'

Kaye had forgotten the box of chocolates that was digging into her ribs under the white fur jacket. She handed the candy over, and Nora's eyes filled with tears. 'Oh, you shouldn't have, my dear girl,' she said. 'But I love them so. How did you know these are my favourite kind?'

Kaye started to correct her, to tell Nora that the chocolates were from Brendan. But he interrupted. 'I cannot tell a lie, Nora,' he said lazily. 'I told Kaye you liked them best.'

Can't tell a lie, my foot, Kaye thought. He had told the strictest sort of truth, but he had certainly managed to leave the impression that the chocolates had been all her idea! Well, perhaps it's easier for him that way, she thought. Nora might feel that she shouldn't accept gifts every time he comes——

Nora opened the box and solemnly offered it around. Brendan crunched a chocolate-dipped almond and told Kaye, his eyes dancing, 'These aren't bad, you know. You have very good taste.'

'I'll think of you every time I eat one, Miss Reardon,' Nora said. She tucked the box under her pillow and sat primly on the edge of the bed. 'I'm so glad you stopped by, Brendan. I hate to bother you on the telephone, but Alma Wiggens told me today that there was a window open on the sun porch. Some careless person who was looking at it left it open, no doubt. I'd have taken care of it myself if I could only get over there to do so, but with the cold——'

'You stay right where you are,' Brendan said. 'I'll stop on my way home and close the window.'

'I'd so like to see it again,' Nora said wistfully.

'I'll take you over some day next spring.'

Kaye was baffled. I haven't the vaguest idea what they're talking about, she thought, and I don't think I should ask.

'You know how careful I always was of it, Brendan,' Nora went on.

There was a harsh knock at the bedroom door. 'Mom says your dinner's ready and to get rid of your company right now,' the teenager said.

Nora's eyes flickered with pain, and then she drew herself up even straighter. Kaye wanted to give her a hug, but she knew any show of sympathy would make it even more difficult for Nora. Her dignity, Kaye thought, was her only defence.

Brendan's jaw set hard, but he said, easily enough, 'I'll see you on Saturday, Nora.'

'You won't forget the window, will you?'

'I'll take care of it right now. You don't mind, do you, Kaye?'

'Of course not,' Kaye said, wondering what it was that she was agreeing to.

'Thank you, dear.' Then Nora's eyes shadowed again, and she asked, almost fearfully, 'Have you had any luck with the platter, Brendan?'

'Oh, I almost forgot about that.'

Kaye's heart was in her throat. The bad news would be another blow to this gallant lady who had already absorbed so much, and she wished there was some way of shielding her from it.

Brendan reached for his wallet. 'The owner of a little shop downtown said she'd never seen anything quite like it.' He pulled out two twenty-dollar bills and handed them to Nora.

Kaye's mouth dropped open. She shut it and concentrated on admiring the way Brendan had got around that one without telling a lie.

Nora gave a long sigh, and then tried to smile. 'I'm so pleased, really I am, my dear,' she said. 'And of course I don't need a platter any more. But—well, it's hard to let go of things like that. I painted it myself when I was just a girl, and I did like it so.'

'I'm sure the new owner will treasure it,' Kaye said gently. 'May I come and visit you again?'

Nora's eyes took on a watery glow. 'I'd be so pleased. But no more chocolates, you hear? When I can't even offer you a glass of water, you shouldn't bring me expensive things.'

'I'll just bring myself,' Kaye promised solemnly. She bit her tongue till they were back in the car, and then she said casually, looking out the window, 'Make sure you don't forget to take that platter out of the back seat before Saturday night.'

'I just couldn't tell her,' Brendan said. He sounded half shy, like a child making a confession.

'For heaven's sake, don't be ashamed of yourself! It would have broken my heart if you'd told her the truth. Where are we going, anyway? What's this about a window and a sun porch?'

'Among the other things Nora lost when she had to give up her convalescent home was her house. She couldn't keep up the mortgage payments, so the bank repossessed it.'

'And she's still trying to take care of it.'

'That's right. The bank has had it listed for sale with my company for eighteen months, so I've been keeping an eye on it.'

'Isn't that an awfully long time for something to be on the market?'

'Not considering the condition of the house.'

The moon was full, and it was only a couple of miles in light traffic from Nora's new house to her old one. They drove through the historic preservation district that included some of the grand old homes of Henderson's history. 'It's in a good neighbourhood, at least,' Kaye said.

Brendan shrugged. 'The street she lived on isn't actually in the preservation area. It could be added to any time, or it could be a slum in twenty years.'

'I suppose you're right,' Kaye said reluctantly.

Brendan swung the car into a gravel driveway where the snow lay in a smooth blanket, unbroken even by footprints. 'It will just take me a second to check the window. Why don't you just wait in the car? No sense in getting out in the snow.'

Kaye looked up at the house, and thought about it. Nora's house was a nineteenth-century Queen Anne, with a shingled tower on one corner and a bay window on the top floor. There were loose clapboards here and there, and the porch floor sagged out of line. It badly needed a coat of paint. And from what Brendan had said, the inside was in even worse condition.

'I think I will,' Kaye said. 'After some of the things I've seen this week, I don't think I can bear to look at another run-down house.'

'It's unpleasant even to walk through it. I'll be back in just a minute.'

It was considerably longer than a minute, and the cold wind seemed to rock the car and creep through the steel to settle in her bones. Kaye saw lights flash on and off in the house; Brendan, she thought, was certainly making a complete inspection. She leaned back in her seat and studied the house through half-closed eyes, thinking about the preservation district. Last summer there had been a neighbourhood celebration here, with walking tours and some of the houses open to visitors, so everyone could see the marvellous work that was going on in these historic old homes.

I'd love to do something like that, Kaye thought. And the houses are certainly big enough—maybe Graham would like something in this neighbourhood. I wonder if Brendan has thought of that——

She was out of the car and plunging through the knee-deep snow before she stopped to think that she was being a little hasty. She could tell Brendan about her brain-storm in five minutes from now, or tomorrow, just as well. But by then she had reached the front porch, so she went on to the front door. It was oak, with an oval panel of bevelled glass, etched in an intricate pattern. Kaye ran an appreciative finger across it, and then went inside, laughing at herself for her own naïve eagerness to tell Brendan her new idea.

He was coming down the stairs. 'What are you doing in here?' he asked lightly. 'You couldn't stand being left out in the cold?'

She giggled and threw out her arms, matching his own teasing attitude. 'Hi, honey, I'm home!' she carolled.

He stopped as if he had suddenly run into a trans-parent wall and looked down at her, and Kaye stopped breathing. His eyes had gone so suddenly dark that there was no blue left in them, and she had never seen quite the same look in another man's face as she saw in Brendan's then. He came down the last few stairs, and across the hall to her, and took her in his arms.

Her heart was madly skipping beats, and her brain was staggering from fear to ecstasy and back.

'You've been asking for this for a week,' he said huskily.

And then there was no reason for her heart to beat—the electric jolt of his kiss was enough to keep her blood flowing. And her brain refused to think at all, merely to feel, as he held her, his mouth alternately demanding and beseeching, seeking and caressing. It seemed to Kaye as if the world had twisted to some new and crazy angle, and the only thing that kept her from spinning out into space was Brendan, holding her crushed against his body, so closely that it seemed there was not room for a whisper between them ...

CHAPTER SEVEN

SANITY returned slowly. 'Good God!' she whispered finally, staring up at him with eyes that were emerald-green with shock. 'You shouldn't have done that, Brendan.'

'*I* shouldn't?' He sounded a little vague, as if he hadn't used his voice in a month or two. 'You're the one who was issuing the come-hither looks, Kaye. I only accepted the invitation.'

Fury bubbled up within her. 'How *dare* you suggest that I asked for that sort of behaviour!'

'If it upsets you so much,' he suggested gently, 'why don't you slap my face and go running out to the car? It might make you feel better.'

Kaye realised that she was not only still in his arms, but still very comfortably pressed against his chest with her hands nestled into the soft tweed of his jacket—the same jacket that had absorbed her tears only a few hours before. 'Look,' she said, 'because I got upset this afternoon and cried all over you doesn't mean that I wanted to be kissed, for heaven's sake.' She pulled away from him, much more slowly than she had intended, and tugged her coat collar up around her throat in an attempt to hide a blush that threatened to consume her.

'If you say so,' Brendan said. He was leaning against the newel post, watching her thoughtfully.

Kaye looked around, eager to find anything to comment about that might make him stop looking at her like that. She felt absolutely naked under that un-blinking blue gaze, and it frightened her. 'Would you stop making a criminal case of it?' she asked desperately. 'It was only a kiss, after all.'

'You're not being very logical, Kaye. First you get upset with me for kissing you, and now you say it wasn't any big deal. I wonder,' he added thoughtfully, 'which way Graham would see it.'

Kaye's heart settled into her toes with a thump. 'You wouldn't dare tell him,' she said in breathless horror, and then could have bitten her tongue off. If she only had the presence of mind to pretend that it didn't matter! Not that Graham would be angry, she told herself desperately, but if Brendan was doing the telling, she could imagine the way it would end up—it certainly wouldn't appear as one innocent kiss, broken off the instant that she realised what she was doing. No, if Brendan told the story, it would be both painstakingly truthful and absolutely misleading...

'Besides,' she said firmly, 'you're the one who started it. I have no responsibility in the matter at all.'

'And I suppose next you'll say that you weren't even co-operating? I've kissed a few women in my life, Kaye, and I know the difference between one who enjoys it and one who doesn't. And you enjoyed it.'

He pushed himself away from the newel post, and Kaye shrank back against the front door. What if he intended to try to prove his point? she wondered fearfully. She was alone and defenceless here, with no one to come to her aid——

'I'd suggest you be more careful with the signals you send in the future,' he said roughly. 'Nora's window wasn't just left open, by the way. It's been broken. I'm going to the basement to look for something to block it up with. Will you be all right here, or do you want to come along and continue your explanation? It's such a charming story.'

She was determined not to react to the sarcasm in his voice. 'I'll be fine here, thanks.'

It was warm in the house, at least, she told herself, and it was going to take a while to fix the window. There was no sense in freezing out in the car. And there was also no sense in standing in the front hall like a hat rack, waiting for him to finish, she told herself. It might leave a wrong impression.

She wandered through the downstairs rooms. At first she scarcely saw them; she was still too upset by that kiss, and his accusation that she had invited it. But eventually the house began to impress itself on her, its elaborately carved woodwork darkened by age, the old and priceless murals water-damaged and hanging loose from the walls of a big sun-room, the carpets stained and splotched. The kitchen was the worst. The ceiling had fallen, and broken plaster lay in heaps over the floor, the old stove, and the sink.

Brendan was coming up the basement stairs with a scrap of lumber. Kaye picked her way through the plaster and stared up into the hole that had been the kitchen ceiling. What looked like new copper pipes spanned the gap.

'What happened to this house?' she asked. 'It looks like a bomb hit it.'

For a moment, she thought he wasn't going to answer. Then he said, 'That's one way to put it. I've also been told that the only way to improve the décor is to bring a bulldozer through.'

There was still a slightly biting tone in his voice, but at least it wasn't directed at her any more, Kaye thought with relief. Everything had returned to normal. 'Surely Nora didn't live here like this——'

'Oh, no. When she moved out, you could see yourself in the wax on the hardwood floors.'

'Then what happened?'

'The bank shut off the boiler last winter to save money and didn't bother to drain the plumbing. The pipes froze and burst and when spring came, there was water all over everything.'

Kaye winced at the thought of gallons of water trickling through the walls and ceilings. 'That was pretty idiotic.'

'It happens. Most of the time, one vice-president doesn't know what the others are up to, so a perfectly saleable house becomes a ghetto in one fast winter.'

'Nora doesn't know about this, does she?' she said slowly.

He shook his head. 'And she isn't going to know, if I can help it.'

'You said you'd bring her over next spring.'

'And next spring I'll come up with another excuse. Why do you think I came myself instead of bringing her over to take care of the window? If she saw her precious house like this, she'd go straight downtown and murder the president of the bank, just to make her point.'

'I'd be cheering her on,' Kaye said. She kicked idly at the broken plaster. The dust from the ceiling had settled into the infinitesimal cracks in the flagstone blocks. It would take a week with a fire hose to scrub it out, she thought.

'Actually,' Brendan said, with an attempt to be scrupulously fair, 'a lot of the damage you see wasn't caused by the water, but by the repairmen. The bank finally concluded that a house without a heating plant isn't in demand, so they replaced the whole thing. But they didn't worry about aesthetics. Wait till you see the upstairs.'

'I'm not certain I want to.' But she followed him up the wide stairway, past a rose-point window that must, she thought, be gorgeous in daylight.

He was right. There was scarcely a room that would be habitable without major work. Ugly brown water stains scarred the ceilings. Wallpaper was falling. Carpets had been pulled up and holes sawed in floors to install new pipes.

'The bulldozer is sounding better and better,' she said.

'It would be criminal,' Brendan said. 'It's still structurally sound—the foundation is in wonderful shape. But try selling this baby. No one wants it.'

'What about you, Brendan?'

'I'm afraid the only future I can see for this house is if someone cuts it into apartments. At least it would earn some of the costs back.'

'I meant that you might want it for yourself. You said you liked Victorian houses.'

'Victorians, yes. Life projects—no, thanks.'

'You just don't like to be tied down,' Kaye accused. 'You want to be free to do whatever strikes your fancy.'

'I am not your father, Kaye. Don't tar me with the same brush.'

She ignored the warning in his voice. 'Doesn't avoiding responsibility get a little old, Brendan?'

He looked for a moment as if he'd really like to slap her. Then he said, 'It hasn't yet. If it ever does, I'll let you know.' He vanished down the hall with his board.

Kaye wandered into a big bedroom. The light fixtures were fantastic, she thought. And the fireplace that was nestled into one corner was surrounded with jade green ceramic tile and topped by a golden oak mantel.

What a shame, she thought, that such a lovely house had been reduced to such a state. Another year and it might not be repairable at all. Nevertheless, even in this state of disarray, the house had something of Nora's own personality—an air of dignity that was no less real for being battered.

Kaye walked through room after room. She wasn't quite sure when she started counting them, and assigning a use to each one. But when she came back into the biggest bedroom, she found herself visualising her choice of wallpaper, her favourite shade of curtains, and the tall four-poster bed that she had always wanted to own, placed just so against the far wall, so that two people could snuggle there and watch a dying fire...

It reminded her of what she had come in to ask Brendan in the first place, before he had started to act bizarre and she had forgotten everything else. She sought him out in the sun porch, where he was fitting the board into the empty spot where the pane of glass had been. The missing pane, she thought, felt almost like a toothache did—a nagging soreness that was always there, reminding her that something was badly wrong under the surface.

'Brendan,' she announced. 'This is a wonderful house.'

'I know,' he muttered. 'You think I should buy it, restore it, and live happily ever after in it, spending the rest of my days patching up roofs and pipes——'

'Not exactly.'

He looked over his shoulder warily, and when he saw the mulish expression on her face, he groaned. 'You're doing it again, Kaye.'

'What?' she demanded. 'Do you think I'm falling blindly in love with another unsuitable house?'

'You took the words right out of my mouth.'

'But I'm not blind to its faults. I know it's got all kinds of things wrong with it. On the other hand, you said yourself that it's solidly built, and all the structural things are fine.'

'I may have said that, but——'

'Look at the space. Look at the high ceilings. Look at the woodwork——'

'Look at the damage.'

'There is that, of course. But it can all be fixed, and when it's finished it will be a beautiful house again—a house to be proud of. I'm sure Graham will think it's worth the investment——'

'Let me get this straight, Kaye. Are you telling me that you plan to ask Graham to buy this house and finance a renovation?'

'Why shouldn't I? He is my fiancé.'

'Oh, I don't know,' he drawled. 'I just thought that you might possibly be doing some thinking about changing that——'

Anger made her stammer just a little. 'Get this straight, Brendan McKenna. One lousy kiss doesn't mean that I'm questioning my engagement.'

'You should do yourself a favour,' he said. 'Before you settle down to Graham, you should check out all your options.'

'And do what? Move in with you? Even if I wasn't going to marry Graham, I'm not about to start playing house with you, Brendan. You're not my type. Have I made myself clear?'

He was standing with arms folded across his broad chest, staring out the window into the darkness. He said finally, 'Perhaps I should remind you, Kaye, that you weren't invited to play house with me.'

It made her furious. 'Pardon me for misunderstanding,' she said with awful politeness. 'Of course I should have realised that you wouldn't tie yourself down to any woman. She might interfere with your fishing!'

'She might try,' he agreed silkily. 'I think it's past time to go home, before this quarrel goes any further. You're tired and emotionally unstable, and you're making no sense at all.'

They didn't exchange a word all the way back to the plaza where Kaye had left her car that afternoon. 'Would you like me to follow you home?' Brendan asked.

'No, thank you,' she said stiffly. 'I wouldn't want to trouble you.'

He nodded. 'I'd think about that house a great deal before you talk to Graham about it,' he said.

She wanted to turn away as if she hadn't heard, but curiosity interfered. He sounded quite matter-of-fact about it now—not angry at all—and she wondered why.

He seemed to read the question in her eyes. 'I don't believe it's Nora's house that you want at all,' he said. 'I think you want an excuse—a long-term project that will postpone the wedding.'

She gasped. 'That is without a doubt the most ridiculous thing anyone has ever said to me.'

'Think about it,' he advised, and his car sped away.

Kaye's apartment was bleak and lonely. She didn't want to go in, she thought as she turned the key. She didn't want to be alone.

Omar came to greet her, but even his welcoming purr had an accusing quality. She sat on the couch in the darkness and stroked the cat's soft white fur and thought about what Brendan had said. 'He's absolutely crazy,' she told Omar. 'To think that I would want to postpone my wedding—to suggest that I might not know what I was doing——' It made her so furious that she squeezed the cat, who protested loudly. 'Sorry, Omar,' she said. 'But the amateur psychologist has it all wrong.'

Nora Farrell's house would not have appealed to her at all, Kaye thought, if she had seen it earlier. It was only after a fruitless search that she was willing to even consider such a project. If, to have the grand house that they wanted, she and Graham had to delay their wedding for a few months, then they would do that. It didn't make it an ideal solution, but it would be worth it in the long run.

Nora Farrell's house had been a home once, and it could be again. It had been beautiful once, and it could be again. With, she told herself honestly, a great deal of work, and money, and time.

She sat there in the dark for nearly an hour, thinking about the house. Away from its atmosphere of decayed charm, and restored to a more realistic frame of mind, she finally admitted the truth to herself. Unless he fell in love with it as she had—a prospect that even Kaye thought was less than likely—Graham would not be willing to put money into a house in that neighbourhood. Brendan had been right about that; the preservation district might reach out to include Nora's street, and it might not. To Graham, it would be a gamble not worth taking, no matter how wonderful the result might be. Nora Farrell's house would probably never return the money invested in it, and so there was no point in even discussing such a project with Graham.

That conclusion did not make her feel at peace. 'I'm the one who will be spending all my time there,' Kaye told Omar. 'Shouldn't I be able to have what I want?'

He stopped purring, and Kaye realised how very self-pitying she must sound. Here she was, complaining about which house she would end up living in, knowing very well that anything Graham agreed to buy would be a showplace—a home any woman in the city would envy her. Meanwhile, there were people like Nora Farrell, who through no fault of her own had been put out of her home and was now reduced to living in a tiny room in a house where she was not even welcome. No one even cared about her except Brendan...

Brendan. Had she been, perhaps, a little too hard on him tonight? He had shown himself to be soft-hearted, and even perhaps a bit sentimental, and after all, it had only been a kiss. Kaye wasn't in the habit of thinking herself irresistible, but maybe they had been spending too much time alone together. Perhaps she had accidentally left him with some mistaken impressions. And as for her own reactions to him—well, the man was certainly attractive. She could hardly be blamed for giving in to that impulse to enjoy being kissed, being held. It certainly didn't mean that there was anything sinister about it.

'If Graham just wasn't so busy this week,' she told Omar, 'it would never have happened at all.' Not that it was Graham's fault, exactly, she told herself hastily. He couldn't help being so very busy at the factory. But she was lonely. Brendan must have felt that, too, and taken it as encouragement.

Not that he had been serious either, Kaye told herself with a flicker of relief. 'One kiss does not lead to anything more serious,' she announced, 'and both of us made that very clear.'

Should she just find another estate agent? That might be the simplest way, but she dreaded the idea of going through all of those preliminaries again. She thought it over and decided that surely nothing so drastic would be necessary. Besides, she reflected, it just didn't seem fair, after Brendan had done all that work, to drop him now and go to someone else.

She'd just have to be more careful when she was around him in the future, she decided, and went to bed with a mind at rest.

Sunday brunch at Claudia's was something of a tra-dition, Graham told Kaye when he came to get her that morning, and Claudia's greeting was almost an echo. 'Graham comes to brunch whenever he can,' Claudia told her. 'Sunday morning is one of the few times when business doesn't intrude.'

'I'm afraid that's the way the business is, Mother. In fact, I have to fly to Colorado tonight. We've got an unacceptable bacteria level in the plant out there, and no one can find out where it's coming from.'

Kaye sipped her tomato juice, and wondered if he meant it was all right for there to be some bacteria in the baby food, as long as it wasn't too much. Better not ask, she told herself. This is not the time to start learning about his business.

'Well, push it to the back of your mind and enjoy your brunch,' Claudia ordered him. 'Why don't you take your skis and have a day's vacation, as long as you have to be out there anyway?'

'Skis?' Graham looked at Claudia as if she was a museum exhibit. 'I've never owned skis, Mother.'

'So rent them.' Claudia turned to Kaye. 'You don't know how much I hope that you can teach this serious son of mine to have a little fun,' she said. 'How is the house-hunting coming along, by the way?'

'Slowly,' Kaye said.

Graham looked at her with a sidelong smile. 'It shouldn't be,' he said. 'You've been spending enough time with your estate agent to find a dozen houses.'

He sounded cheerful enough, but Kaye was uneasy. 'Yes, I have,' she said, trying to keep her voice light. 'But there was something wrong with each one of them. So we kept looking.'

'At Maxie's Bar? Angela Warren told me she saw you there with him one afternoon.'

Kaye had almost forgotten the incident. 'Oh, that,' she said casually, horribly aware that Claudia's sapphire eyes were fixed on her with silent interest. 'Brendan and I thought we'd found the perfect house that day—you know, the one in Henderson Heights that you thought was too small. We were going to celebrate when we ran into Angela——' It sounded like a pathetic excuse, she thought. And the fact that it was absolutely true didn't make her feel less guilty. You should have told him earlier, she lectured herself. Angela Warren was a notorious gossip, determined always to know every detail of every story. It was inevitable that she would have mentioned it to Graham. 'I've had lunch with him a couple of times, too,' she added stiffly.

Graham gave her an indulgent smile. 'I'm only teasing, Kaye. Surely you don't think I'm the jealous sort, do you?'

'Of course not,' she said. She should feel better, she told herself. Of course Graham wasn't jealous. But then, he didn't know everything, either. He didn't know that she'd had waffles at Brendan's apartment last Sunday morning, and he didn't know about that kiss——

Stop it, she told herself. There was nothing important about either of those things, and there was nothing for Graham to be jealous of.

'Though as far as houses are concerned,' Graham said, 'I'm beginning to think I'll have to take a hand in it if we're ever going to get anywhere.'

'I wish you would,' Kaye said. At least then he would understand the frustration, she thought.

'I will when I get back,' he said. 'There are a couple that Andy Winchester thinks might be quite satisfactory. I just don't quite trust this man of yours, Kaye, though I do understand now why he sells houses and not commercial real estate. It's because his charm works better when he's dealing with emotional people instead of businessmen.'

Kaye thought that one over. Before she could quite decide whether she had been insulted, the maid set an omelette before her. Steam rose gently from the golden-brown surface, curling around the red rose that garnished the plate.

'In all the planning for a house,' Claudia said, 'don't forget that as soon as you've set a date we'll have to get started on the wedding plans. I don't suppose you've given a thought to your china and crystal patterns. And if you're to have a really wonderful trip, you'll have to make reservations soon.'

'I've been thinking about it,' Graham said. 'If we were to go to Europe, I could visit some of the manufacturers over there, and perhaps bring home some improvements——'

'Graham,' his mother said flatly. 'Honeymoons should not be turned into business trips. Don't you think you should ask Kaye where she'd like to go?'

Kaye took a thoughtful bite of her omelette and thought about it. 'The Bahamas,' she said dreamily. She had always wanted to see the Caribbean, but this winter the dream had grown steadily stronger, until it was almost a hunger.

'The Bahamas?' Graham sounded disbelieving. 'But it will be summer, Kaye.'

I'm not so sure, she reflected. If we don't find a house soon, it might be next winter before we're married. And Brendan thinks that I wouldn't care if it was next year, she reminded herself. Well, Brendan was wrong.

'Why the Bahamas, anyway?' he asked.

'I suppose it's because there's a travel agency in town offering a one-day tour. It's been hard not to think about Nassau when I hear about it all the time.'

Claudia wrinkled her nose thoughtfully. 'One day? That would scarcely give you a taste of the island.'

'You're right, of course,' Kaye said. 'But it's a package that even I could afford, except that I've been taking so much time off work lately to look at houses.'

'Go,' Graham said. 'Get it out of your system. I don't find the idea very appealing, myself, but if that's the kind of thing you like——'

'I told you,' Kaye said. 'I can't afford it right now. My last pay cheque was a little sparse.'

Graham smiled. 'Darling, you don't think that really matters? I know you're not earning much at that agency, and of course you'll have to stop working even before the wedding.'

'What do you mean, *of course*?'

He looked startled. 'I fully expect to take care of your outstanding bills when we're married, Kaye. For sensible things,' he added quickly. 'Living expenses. Don't go charging any diamond necklaces to me, now, just because I said I'd pay your debts.'

For an instant, she wasn't quite sure that she had heard correctly. The words seemed to ring through her head, and fury boiled up in her. So he's going to take care of my debts, is he? she thought. I suppose I should accept that as a generous compliment, but I'm afraid I can't.

'I don't have any debts, Graham.' She kept her voice level with an effort. 'I don't believe in relying on anyone to rescue me from my own foolishness, and I have every intention of keeping my job and earning my own spending money for a while, at least. And as for the idea that I would have the nerve to go charge mink coats and trips to the Caribbean to you before we're married——' Despite her best intentions, her voice was rising.

Claudia intervened. 'Of course you wouldn't, Kaye,' she said. 'And Graham, while it's very thoughtful of you to help Kaye out financially because she's taking time off work to look for a house, you must respect her desire to be independent.'

Graham looked a bit sulky, as if he didn't have the least idea why Kaye would be angry at his generous gesture.

'But perhaps you could give her this trip,' Claudia went on.

'I couldn't take it,' Kaye said. 'To take a trip promoted by another travel agency would be grounds for losing my job.'

'Are you certain of that?' Claudia asked.

'No. I mean, Marilyn hasn't actually said that. But I can't imagine that she'd like it, and I wouldn't even want to ask.'

'In any case, I wasn't really thinking of that trip,' Claudia said. 'You'd want three days at least, and better yet a week. Surely your own agency could make arrangements——'

'With the house-hunting and everything, I don't think it would be a good idea to ask for that much time off right now,' Kaye said. 'I guess I'll have to wait till next winter.' She tried to smile. 'Besides, I'd have to make some sort of arrangements for my cat if I was going to be gone that long.' Claudia looked interested, and Kaye went on, 'He's a Persian who doesn't like being left alone.'

'He's a spoiled-rotten animal,' Graham announced.

Kaye looked at him in astonishment. He'd never actually said anything about Omar before. It sounded as if he hated the cat, but surely that couldn't be it. Graham must just be sulking about her refusal to take money from him.

Graham went on, 'He has been allowed to think that house plants are vegetables, and human ankles are an acceptable source of protein.'

'That's not true,' Kaye said. 'If you'd just make an effort to get to like him——'

'What about him getting to like me? The next time that animal takes a swipe at me, I'm going to turn him into a Persian rug. You could at least get him de-clawed, Kaye——'

'It's cruel to do that. And he's well-trained; he doesn't scratch furniture.'

'You haven't got any furniture worth protecting,' Graham said.

There was some truth to that, Kaye reflected; most of her furniture was strictly bargain-basement fare. Of course, it isn't as if Graham is abnormal, she told herself. Some people like cats, others don't. I wouldn't like to live with an alligator, myself, and if Graham owned one, I might be making noises about turning it into a handbag and shoes. To him, the cat is no different.

Perhaps the sensible thing to do was to find another home for Omar, she thought. If it came to a choice between her cat and her future husband, Omar would—of course—have to go.

Poor Omar, she thought. I wonder what will happen to you, and if you'll break your heart in a new home, wanting to come back to me.

CHAPTER EIGHT

EMILY put the telephone back in its cradle, cleared the computer screen of the airline schedules she had been checking on, leaned back in her chair and thoughtfully looked across the office at Kaye. 'What's wrong with you this morning?' she said finally.

Kaye jumped, and looked up from the papers spread on her desk. 'Are you talking to me?'

'No, I'm asking the computer if it has indigestion. Of course I'm talking to you. You look as if you haven't slept all weekend. Is something wrong between you and Graham?'

Kaye shook her head. 'Of course not. He's out of town, though. He left last night.'

'And even when he's here, he's absorbed in business. You know, my mother always told me it was just as easy to fall in love with a rich man as a poor one, but sometimes I wonder if she was right.'

Kaye's temper flared. 'My engagement has got nothing to do with Graham's money, Emily,' she snapped.

'Don't bite my head off. All I said was, the schedule that man works is absolutely iniquitous. When are you ever going to see him?'

'It will be different when we're married.' Kaye wished that she felt as serene about that as she sounded.

'What an innocent you are. How old are you, Kaye?'

'Twenty-three.'

'And you haven't found out yet that men don't change just because women want them to?'

'You're such a cynic, Emily.'

'I have a right to be. I learned it the old-fashioned way—by experience. Kaye, are you really certain you want to go through with this? Are you positive this is right for you?'

Why is it, Kaye asked herself irritably, that everyone is so sceptical about my engagement? First Brendan, and now Emily as well—and even Claudia had looked a little doubtful yesterday. Of course, who could blame her? They had almost come to blows at her breakfast table.

'I am certain,' she said, and could have bitten her tongue off because her voice quivered a little.

Emily looked at her thoughtfully for a long moment, and then said, 'If you're going to marry Graham because of his money, at least don't try to kid yourself about being in love with him. It will only make it harder on you——'

'I am not marrying him for his money!'

'I'm not so sure.'

'Well, I'm not foolish enough to think that people can live on love alone. I want a little financial security.'

'Why?' Emily asked reasonably. 'You've lived without it this long.'

'Yes, and I don't like it. The idea of going off on a fishing trip without knowing or caring whether next month's bills will be paid——' Her voice was scathing.

'Which fisherman are we talking about?' After a long silence, Emily said, on a long note, 'Oh. Now I think I understand.'

Kaye said crossly, 'And just what marvellous insight have you achieved into my wounded psyche this time?'

'You'd better get Brendan McKenna out of your mind, you know. It isn't healthy to be thinking about that handsome Irishman all the time.'

'What makes you think he's even in my mind?' Kaye knew she sounded sharp, and she didn't care.

'That is who you meant, isn't it?'

Kaye bit her lip. Finally, she nodded. She hadn't talked to Brendan in three days, since they had quarrelled that night in Nora Farrell's house, but she had been thinking of him, and she had to admit that it wasn't very pleasant to have Emily almost reading her thoughts. 'He's utterly crazy when it comes to money,' she said finally. 'He says the future doesn't matter as long as you enjoy today, and a lot of garbage like that.'

Emily watched her for a long moment. 'Well, I don't notice the sheriff being after him for not paying his bills,' she observed finally. 'And his philosophy of life might not be exactly your ideal, but it sounds like a lot more fun than pinching pennies.' After a moment, Emily asked quietly, 'Do you know what puzzles me, Kaye? Why are you taking it so personally? If you think Brendan McKenna is a fool about money, why not just ignore him, and let him go to the devil in his own chosen way? What does it matter to you?'

Good question, Kaye thought. Why didn't she just laugh at Brendan's ideas and go on about her own life? It certainly wasn't going to affect her if his car payments weren't made on time. So why did it matter?

'If you want my opinion, I think he's crept into your heart,' Emily said.

'Crept into my—Emily, are you saying I've fallen in love with him?'

'Not necessarily. But he's certainly attractive, and he's been dancing attendance on you for two weeks. It wouldn't be any surprise if you had let yourself become infatuated with him.'

Kaye thought about that one. Had she developed sort of a little-girl crush on Brendan McKenna? The idea made a frightening kind of sense. It accounted for all sorts of things, the kiss in Nora's front hall among them.

'Don't be ridiculous,' she protested. 'I can't be infatuated with him. I'm engaged.'

'Be honest with yourself, Kaye. Do you look forward to seeing him? Does your heart skip kind of funny when you answer the phone and it's him? Do you find yourself thinking of things you want to tell him?'

Kaye bit her lip. 'Yes,' she whispered.

'Infatuation,' Emily said triumphantly. 'Nothing serious, of course. It will pass, with time. Of course, if you want to get over it sooner——'

Kaye hated herself for taking the bait, but she asked, 'What do you think I should do about it, oh, great adviser?'

'Have a fling with him,' Emily said promptly. 'There is nothing that will end an infatuation faster than to indulge it. I've done it myself a dozen times.'

Kaye's voice cracked. 'A dozen?'

'Don't sound so horrified. I wasn't speaking literally.'

'I should hope not. Thanks for the advice, Emily, but I think I'll just let it wear itself out—*if* it is an infatuation after all, and not merely being bored with winter. I'm just not the type to go around having an affair with any man I find mildly attractive.' Kaye turned back to the itinerary she was preparing for a client's car tour of the South.

But her mind wasn't on the tour. For an instant, the travel agency faded away completely, and she could see Brendan's face, hear his voice, feel the warmth of his mouth on hers, as surely as if she was back in the front hall of Nora's house, in his arms. Have a fling, Emily had said lightly. It was a casual, playful term for something that would be neither. Emily might be able to indulge herself that way; Kaye could not. An affair for her would be an emotionally searing experience, something that would forever change her——

And, feeling that way, how could she even consider doing anything of the sort?

My God, she thought. Just what is it about Brendan McKenna, anyway? What black magic is there about the man that could tempt me to risk everything I've hoped and dreamed of?

He was certainly handsome, and charming, and fun to talk to; so were a lot of other men, but she hadn't felt any particular desire for them. It is quite ridiculous to be feeling this way, she thought. Having an affair with Brendan McKenna would be a first-class disaster, a heedless gamble against breathtaking odds. And at the end, what? Certainly there would be hurt, and anger, and pain, and loss. Don't forget the loss, she reminded. Because it's Graham you would be losing...

You've obviously got a self-destructive gene, Kaye told herself. You must have inherited it from your father, and you've never even known it was there. It's fortunate for you that you met Graham first—steady, dependable Graham—before you ran into Brendan McKenna...

'The next best thing would be to leave town for a while,' Emily went on.

'I'd love to,' Kaye said absently. 'What do you suggest?'

'How about a free ticket to the Bahamas?'

Kaye put her pencil down. 'You are full of surprises this morning, aren't you? What is this, a contest?'

'No. A friend of mine turned traitor and bought a ticket for the one-day jaunt from our competition. She's supposed to go tomorrow. However, poetic justice caught up with her—she fell down her basement steps last night and broke her leg. She called me last night and confessed what she'd done, and told me I could have the ticket.'

'So why aren't you going?'

'I can't. There's a school function that I can't miss. Besides, it would take me three months of dieting before I could show myself on the beach. Do you want to go?'

'Marilyn would fire me in a minute flat.'

'No, she wouldn't. In any case, she doesn't need to know. I'll tell her tomorrow morning that you called in sick——'

'If she finds out, I won't have to pretend to be sick— and I'll be out of a job, too.'

'When you come back, you can tell her all the details about how they make that trip work. They have to be cutting corners somehow to do it at that price— I certainly can't figure it out, and I don't think Marilyn understands it either.'

'You mean, go as a spy?' Stranger things had happened, Kaye told herself. 'The promoters won't be pleased.'

'They probably won't even recognise you,' Emily pointed out. 'Wear your dark glasses, and you'll be just one more tourist on the plane. How could anyone object, anyway?'

'Marilyn could.'

Emily looked irritated. 'Kaye, you are the most rigid person I know,' she said disgustedly.

The front door opened and Marilyn came in, swinging her briefcase. Emily looked across at Kaye with raised eyebrows, as if to say that she'd never seen the boss in that frame of mind before.

Marilyn tossed her coat over a chair. 'Kaye, you're an absolute darling,' she said, and Emily's eyebrows went even higher. 'I wanted you to be the first to know— I've just bought a house, and it's all because of you.'

'Me?' Kaye said weakly.

'Yes. You and that handsome young man you recommended. He's such a charmer, isn't he? He won't stop
at anything to clinch a deal.'

I hadn't found him to be quite that way, Kaye thought.
With me, he seems to want to talk me out of every house
I find appealing. Or is he just using reverse psychology
on me?

'At any rate, he showed me that house you liked so
well in Henderson Heights—the one with the perfectly
awful pink carpet. And I fell in love with it. I just found
out this morning that the owners have accepted my offer.'

'It's huge, Marilyn. I thought you were looking for a
smaller place——'

'Kaye, darling, who ever said that buying a house was
a time to be practical?'

There was no arguing with that. My house, Kaye
thought with a sudden pang. That beautiful modern
house hanging over the still, snow-swept valley. But she
was surprised that it was only a twinge of pain, and not
an agonising torment.

'See?' Emily said in a conspiratorial whisper, once
Marilyn had gone to her office. 'She's in such a good
mood she wouldn't get angry at you, no matter what
you did.'

'I'm not so sure,' Kaye said. But she had to admit
that Emily's offer was tempting. A day on the beach,
to bake in the warm rays of the southern sun and to
think—to get her mind straightened out and banish this
ridiculous notion of Emily's that she should have an
affair with Brendan in order to forget him.

And the trip would be free, at that—the ticket would
not drain even the tiniest amount from her carefully
hoarded savings.

'Are you positive that you don't want to use that ticket
yourself?' she asked finally.

Emily nodded. 'I'm certain. If you don't go, Kaye, it will be wasted—I can hardly call up anyone else and ask if they want to travel with our competition.'

'That's true.' With sudden decision, Kaye said, 'Very well, I'll go. But only if Marilyn approves.'

Emily looked startled. 'Why risk it? She might say no.'

Emily, Kaye thought, had an underdeveloped sense of ethics. 'Because I'm no good at faking illness,' she said. 'If I tried to pretend I was coming down with a cold, I'd accidentally give myself a sore throat and have to stay home, and that really would be a disaster.'

Brendan called about the middle of the afternoon, and Kaye was proud of her calm tone when she greeted him. 'It's been days since I heard from you,' she said. 'I was beginning to wonder if you wanted to drop the whole thing.'

'Funny. I was wondering the same thing about you.'

His voice was husky and warm, and it started doing drastic things to Kaye's backbone. She said hastily, 'Of course not. It would be pretty senseless of me to start all over with another agent, don't you think?'

There was a long pause, and then he said, 'Actually, that wasn't what I called you about. I don't have any houses lined up for you to look at, just now.'

'I understand that you've been busy with Marilyn's purchase.'

'Do you mind? I know how much you liked that house.'

'That's life,' Kaye said with a shrug, and was a little surprised to find that she meant it. 'Since I couldn't have it, I'm glad someone else wanted it. She's very pleased with you.'

'As a matter of fact, I think I should split the commission with you,' Brendan said.

'Why?'

'Because you did more selling than I did. I just walked through with her—she'd already fallen in love with it from your description.'

'With everything except the pink carpet,' Kaye laughed. 'Brendan, I couldn't possibly accept money for what I did. Sending my friends to you is the least I can do, since I can't seem to find a house myself.'

'Then I'd like to take you to dinner to say thank you.'

And run into someone like Angela Warren, who would promptly tell Graham all about her evening out? Not that there was anything to hide, but still—— 'I don't think that would be such a wise idea.'

'There's nothing to be frightened of, Kaye.' There was a long silence, and then he said, 'I wanted to tell you that I'm sorry for what happened at Nora's house. I was reading the signals wrong, and I'm very sorry I made you uncomfortable.'

'It's——' She cleared her throat, and said, 'It was nothing.'

'I'd like to get things back to normal. We've pretty much exhausted the houses I had in mind, and I really don't know where to look next. I'm tied up with a client all afternoon, but if we start over tonight with the multiple listings books, by the end of the week we can be searching again.'

Kaye sighed. If there was anything she didn't want to do, it was to look through all those books again, with their blindingly small print and tiny, greyish photographs—pictures that made all the houses look the same. But he sounded determined, and after all, she wanted this search to be finished just as much as he did.

'All right,' she said. 'I'll look at the books tonight. But not over dinner, Brendan.'

'Why? Would Graham object?'

She didn't answer that. I don't have to explain it, she told herself. 'Why don't you just bring the books over when you're finished with your client?'

'All right,' he said finally. 'It would be about six o'clock, I think.'

'That's fine. I'll be at home.'

Emily was watching her with an approving smile. 'So you're taking my advice,' she said cheerfully. 'Inviting him over for a cosy evening in your little place. You've got better sense than I thought, except for one thing— you have to be at the airport by five in the morning. It doesn't leave much time to enjoy——'

'I'm not planning on losing any sleep over Brendan McKenna,' Kaye said tartly.

Emily just shook her head regretfully.

Kaye stopped on the way home and bought a bottle of wine. It couldn't hurt to offer him a drink.

The little store was only a few blocks from Nora Farrell's old house. Kaye drove slowly down the street, letting the car creep foot by foot past the big, dark house with the tower. It looked, in the dim moonlight, like a perfect setting for a haunted house tour.

What a shame, she thought. If Nora had been able to stay there, the house would still be a useful part of society. Now it, and Nora, were both lonely, without a place or a function.

She glanced at her watch and turned towards the street of bungalows where Nora lived now. It was nearly an hour till Brendan would come to her apartment, and something impelled her to stop and see that gallant old lady.

The same teenager answered the door. It seemed to Kaye that the same movie was flickering on the television set, and the same dishes were piled around the couch. The teenager recognised her and jerked a thumb towards Nora's room. She found her way along the dim hall and knocked.

'Miss Reardon,' Nora said. There was a note of wonder in the cultured old voice, and Kaye had to choke back tears as she stooped to kiss Nora's wrinkled cheek. 'How I wish I still lived in my own house,' the old woman said. 'I would like to offer you tea in my drawing-room.'

There was no self-pity in her voice, merely the wish that her guest could be properly entertained. Kaye forced herself to smile and play along. 'With a fire crackling,' she said, 'and a cat asleep on the hearth rug——'

'Did Brendan tell you that I used to have cats?'

'No, but I thought it would make a beautiful sight.'

'I miss my babies,' Nora said dreamily. 'They were always just cats—nothing pure-bred about them, I'm afraid. Mostly they were strays who found their way to me and stayed. But they all got old, and died.' She sighed. 'It's just as well. I couldn't have brought them here, and I never could have sent them back out into the cold.'

Kaye shivered at that thought herself. Where was she to find another home for Omar? she wondered. She could feel confident about handing him over to someone like Nora, but there was no chance of that.

She pushed the thought away. She certainly hadn't come here to start Nora mourning her lost pets. 'We could pretend,' she said lightly, and pantomimed lifting a cup to her lips. 'What a lovely, light fragrance this tea has, Miss Farrell!'

Nora smiled faintly. 'They'd say I was having delusions,' she said. 'And they'd lock me up.'

It was a small thing, really, but it made Kaye furious. How dared they take away even the woman's daydreams, she thought. There must be an answer. Somewhere, in a city of a hundred thousand people, there must be an agency that could help Nora Farrell. It was just too cruel that in a town this size there could be such a brutal difference in how people lived. How unfair it was, Kaye told herself, that Claudia Forrest had her huge penthouse apartment, her maid, her furs, and her fresh flowers, when Nora had so little.

Perhaps Claudia would help, Kaye thought. She's human—she cares about people. She would feel sympathy for Nora's plight.

'I miss my house so much,' Nora said. There was a twinge of pain in her voice. 'If I could only see it again, I'd feel better. But I'm afraid Brendan won't take me to see it. He tells me he will, but I don't think he means it.'

Kaye closed her eyes, thinking in despair of the horrifying difference between Nora's house as she remembered it and the way it was today. 'I'm sure he will, when he can,' she said doubtfully. 'There are reasons, I'm sure——'

'Will you take me? You have a car.'

'Nora, I can't possibly do that, and anyway, we couldn't get inside. The house has a lockbox on the door—you know, the ones that estate agents put on so only they can get the key——'

Nora was shaking her head. 'We don't need their key.'

Kaye said, weakly, 'What do you mean?' She had a momentary vision of Nora Farrell in her neat navy-print house dress and old-fashioned black shoes climbing over the sill of the pantry window.

Then she realised that there was a much simpler explanation. 'Nora,' she demanded, 'do you still have a key to that house?'

Nora seemed to debate something within herself, but finally she nodded, like a small child who has just been caught in mischief. 'If you won't take me,' she said with decision, 'and Brendan won't, then I'll just have to do something about it myself when the weather is better and I can walk over there.'

'Nora!' Kaye was horrified. If the old lady carried out this mad plan, and walked in to see the devastation of her beloved house—well, the next estate agent who came to show it was apt to find a tiny, fragile body somewhere inside, dead of a heart attack. But how on earth could she be stopped? Kaye wondered frantically.

'Nora, you can't use that key,' she said hoarsely. 'It— it would get Brendan into trouble. They would think that he had known all along that you had it.'

Nora blinked. 'They would?' she said doubtfully.

Kaye plunged on. 'It would be awful for him. They might even think that he'd told you that you could go there.' She paused, and added, more gently, 'I know it's hard to accept, but the bank does own the house now, Nora, and you'd be trespassing if you went there alone. And if they thought Brendan knew you were doing it——'

'Trespassing?' Nora repeated.

There was a long silence.

'You wouldn't want to make trouble for Brendan, would you?'

Nora shook her head.

'I think Brendan should have the key,' Kaye said. 'Why don't you give it to me now? I'm seeing him tonight, and I'll explain about it.'

'He won't be angry with me?' Nora said tremulously. 'I didn't ever use it. I just wanted to have it, in case. I didn't understand that it might make trouble for him.'

'He won't be angry.' Kaye had never been so certain of anything in her life. Brendan might be horrified at this narrow escape from disaster, or relieved to have the phantom key back where it belonged. He would be anything but angry. Brendan didn't get angry, she reflected, remembering the night she had put the dent in his car. They had stood there in the snow that night, together, as if nothing else in the world existed... She dragged her attention ruthlessly back to the moment. No daydreams, she warned herself.

Nora sighed. Then she turned to the little chest beside her bed and peeled a small envelope from the underside of the top drawer, where it had been taped. She held it for a few seconds, and then handed it across to Kaye. 'You'll explain it to him?'

'Of course I will.' Kaye received the key thankfully and put it in the innermost pocket of her handbag, where it couldn't possibly disappear.

'And you'll tell him how much I'd like to see my house?' Nora asked wistfully. 'I don't think he believes it would be good for me, but it would be just like medicine to walk through my house one more time.'

'I'll tell him,' Kaye whispered. 'I have to go, Nora. I'll stop and see you again.'

'Please do,' Nora said with dignity. 'I won't be such a weak-kneed female next time. I detest old people who feel sorry for themselves because times have changed, and I hate it when I sound like one of them.'

Kaye was quite proud of herself for holding back the tears till she reached her car. By the time she reached her own apartment, she had re-established her self-control, and some cold water on her face and a few

minutes with her make-up kit made her feel much better.
As soon as she got back from her day in the sun, she
told herself, she would start burning up the telephone
lines until someone in authority found a better solution
for Nora. There had to be one; she was convinced of
that.

Brendan was late, and she found herself pacing the
floor as she waited for him. Do you look forward to
seeing him? Emily had asked. Do you find yourself
thinking of things you want to tell him?

'Oh, stop it,' Kaye told herself angrily. 'He's a nice
guy and you've spent a lot of time with him lately; that's
all there is to it. You just have to get control of yourself.'

But when the doorbell rang she jumped up so quickly
that Omar tumbled from her lap and sprawled on the
floor. He picked himself up and looked at her accusingly, but Kaye was already at the door.

Brendan handed her a bag. 'Dinner,' he said. 'I didn't
think it was appropriate for us to starve.'

She sniffed. 'Smells good.'

'Barbecued ribs from the place on LeGrange
Boulevard.'

'You disappoint me,' she teased. 'I thought you'd
rushed home and cooked them yourself. Come in.'

He put a stack of books on the corner of the coffee-
table, and Kaye looked at them with distaste. 'Food first,'
she decreed. 'This apartment doesn't accommodate elegant dining, I'm afraid. How about having a picnic in
the middle of the floor?'

'Sounds good to me.' Brendan tossed his jacket over
the arm of the couch, loosened his tie, and sank down
on to the carpet with a sigh.

'I'll get the wine. It's white, I'm afraid—not quite the
thing to go with ribs.'

'Let's be crass and drink it anyway.' He didn't sound as if he cared. 'It has been a very long day, and I could stand a drink before we start looking at those books again.'

'Don't you have them memorised by now?'

'Nearly. I know every five-bedroom house in Henderson by sight, that's sure.'

'Look on the bright side,' she suggested. 'Every time you show me a house, Brendan, you earn another gold star in your heavenly crown—for patience and things like that.'

'Honey, this has become a personal quest, you know.' But he wasn't emphatic about it—he sounded tired instead, she thought.

She handed him the wine bottle and a corkscrew. 'I'll set the table while you pour.' She spread a blanket out over the carpet and unpacked the bag he had brought.

The food was good—the ribs were firm and heavily coated in sauce, and yet with the first touch, the meat peeled exquisitely off the bones and almost melted in her mouth. 'I have to give you credit,' she said finally, as she set her plate aside. 'You can certainly choose a restaurant.'

She looked at the stack of books on the coffee-table and sighed. Sooner or later, she thought, I will have to start, and I might as well not take up any more of the man's time than necessary. He looks exhausted tonight.

She unfolded herself from her cross-legged position and picked up the plates. He didn't offer to help, which surprised her, and when she came back a few minutes later with a warm wet towel to get rid of the barbecue sauce, he had stretched out full length on the floor. His eyes were closed and one brown hand lay across Omar's white fur, as if he had gone to sleep in the middle of petting the animal.

Kaye's hand clenched hard on the towel, as she tried to fight off the urge to forget all about the sticky barbecue sauce and just creep silently between him and the cat. What would it be like to lie there with him, she wondered, nestled against his body, with his hands petting and massaging her——

Don't be an idiot, she told herself. You're an engaged woman——

But if you feel this way about another man, a still small voice in the back of her brain reminded, perhaps you shouldn't be...

CHAPTER NINE

BRENDAN moved then, and stretched as gracefully as a cat. 'What you need,' he said without opening his eyes, 'is a fireplace, Kaye. A nice log fire on a cold night like this would be the finishing touch in comfort.'

'I'm looking for one. Remember?' To her own ears, her voice sounded oddly strained, but he didn't seem to notice anything unusual.

'I'm doing the best I can,' he said lightly. 'It's not my fault you're impossible to please. I can think of a dozen nice fireplaces you've turned down, just because you didn't like the houses they were attached to.'

That should put you in your place, Kaye told herself, and show you what a silly goose you're being. It's apparent that he isn't suffering from any romantic notions. All he had had in mind that night in Nora's front hall, Kaye told herself, was a bit of dalliance with a willing client. Marilyn had been right; he would do anything to sell a house, but he had simply misread Kaye. As soon as she had made it clear that she wasn't interested, that was the end of that—Brendan McKenna wasn't about to endanger a commission to get a little fun on the side.

I should be happy that he revealed himself so clearly, she told herself. And I am. I'm very glad indeed.

'Here's a wet towel to wipe off the barbecue sauce,' she said, and dropped it beside him. She looked longingly at the blanket—it had nothing to do with him, she thought; it was just that the floor was her favourite place to stretch out and read—and then settled herself on the couch with the heavy books.

'Omar thanks you,' Brendan said lazily. 'I accidentally petted him with sauce on my hand, and got it all over his fur. We mere humans have no idea what a terrible job it is to be a Persian cat, you know.'

'I'd like to try it some time. Napping on a pillow all day——'

'And having to eat canned cat food?'

'That would be a drawback.' Kaye turned automatically to the section of the multiple listing book that showed large homes. She looked down at the first page of grainy photographs with distaste. 'I know you've sort of got Sultan for a pet,' she began, remembering the huge orange cat she had found on his front porch the day he had made waffles for her.

'Or Sultan sort of has me,' Brendan agreed.

'I don't suppose you'd want a full-time cat, would you?'

'Why? Have you got a stray in the neighbourhood?'

'No. I'm looking for a new home for Omar.'

'I know of a nice little two-bedroom bungalow——' He saw the flash in her eyes. 'Sorry, Kaye. Why are you giving away your cat?'

The details of her decision were really none of his business, she decided. 'Because I'm gone so much, and he isn't used to strangers.'

'That makes no sense at all. You'll be home more once you've found a house, and how can you give him away if he doesn't like new people?'

'Well, you needn't sound so horridly suspicious of my motives,' she said tartly. 'There is absolutely nothing wrong with him. Besides, he's a purebred, and you wouldn't believe what they cost.'

'That sort of thing never weighed heavily with me. I've seen a lot of alley cats who had more personality than the highly bred darlings.'

'Don't take offence, Omar,' she said drily. 'I'm sure he didn't mean it personally. I thought you might like to have him, Brendan. You two certainly seem to get along well enough.'

'That's true. And I'm a stranger—which only confirms my feeling that you haven't given the real reason.'

'If you don't want him, just say so. And in that case, it certainly isn't necessary to probe my reasons.'

'But it is fun, isn't it?' He propped himself up on one elbow and absently scratched Omar's chin. 'I'll bet that the stranger he doesn't get along with is Graham. Am I right?'

She turned another page, jotted down another address on what was promising to be a very short list, and tried to ignore him.

'Your silence confirms my opinion,' Brendan pointed out.

What did it matter? she asked herself. 'Graham doesn't care for cats, that's all. It's a matter of taste—I wouldn't like to have a python running around the house, myself.'

'Why don't you just keep Omar and get rid of Graham? A python would be a warm fuzzy compared to him.'

'I do not want to hear any more of your nasty comments——'

'Besides,' Brendan went on smoothly, 'you can't give a cat away as you would an old sweater you don't wear any more. Omar wouldn't understand.'

'I don't see that I have much choice, Brendan. I've let Omar get very spoiled, and he is horribly jealous of Graham, that's all. He's too old to change, and it would be cruel to make him live with someone he doesn't like——'

'Oh, too true.'

Kaye eyed him warily, but Brendan looked angelically innocent. Omar rolled over and Brendan started to scratch the cat's stomach. Omar stretched luxuriously and his purr grew so loud that Kaye could hear it half-way across the room.

'He's used to having things his own way,' she went on. 'If I was to come down on the floor with you right now, he'd be so jealous and obnoxious that he'd probably claw you to pieces.'

Brendan patted the blanket. 'Come on. Let's see.'

'I was only using that as an illustration,' Kaye said stiffly.

'I know. But I'm inspecting a possible life's companion here. I don't want any unpleasant surprises after I get him home.'

'You're serious? You might take him?'

'I might. Come on down and let's see what happens.'

'No, thanks.'

'Are you scared?' he said softly. 'Of me?'

'Of course not. But I'd appreciate it if you didn't make any more tasteless jokes about it.' She turned a page, having seen nothing that was on it. Her fingers were trembling. She couldn't look at him.

'I beg your pardon.' His voice was harsh.

She nodded stiffly. For the next few minutes, there was no sound in the room except for pages turning. Omar had stopped purring, as if he recognised the tension be-tween them.

Or was the tension only in herself? Kaye wondered. Brendan was still sprawled on the floor with one forearm over his eyes; he looked as if he was asleep. Apparently it was only she who was uncomfortable. And why should that be? she asked herself. Why should he have such tremendous power to upset her, to make her feel like a nervous schoolgirl?

She studied him with an attempt at scientific detachment. Emily was right about him being good-looking; even stretched out on the floor asleep he was one of the handsomest men she had ever seen. Her hand went out half-consciously to caress the rough fibres of his grey herringbone jacket, where he had flung it over the arm of the couch. It smelled ever so slightly of his aftershave.

His face was lean and relaxed at the moment. The mouth that could quirk in a sudden grin was unsmiling now. She couldn't see his eyes, but she could still picture them in her mind—so dark blue that they sometimes looked black, and yet never quite without that wicked sparkle that promised a teasing for someone . . .

'Have I passed inspection?' he asked lazily.

Kaye sucked in a long, startled breath and dropped her eyes to the book in her lap, willing herself not to change colour. 'I don't know what you mean,' she said, as coolly as she could.

'Oh?' He sat up. 'I could have sworn you were watching me.'

'Do you often have delusions that you're being stared at?' she asked crisply.

He grinned. 'Only when there's a pretty girl in the room. What are you finding in the books?'

'Not much.' It was a relief to have the subject changed, she thought, and then had second thoughts when he came across to the couch to see for himself.

'Mind if I move this?' he murmured, and gently unclenched her hand from the sleeve of his jacket so he could lay it aside.

I was hanging on to it like a life preserver, Kaye thought incredulously; how perfectly embarrassing that he caught me doing it! She had lost the battle to keep from blushing.

He leaned over her shoulder; she shifted nervously away. 'Now, show me what you've found.'

She turned pages with tremulous hands, and leaned towards him to point out a photograph. 'I thought that one was pretty.'

'Lovely,' he said.

She waited for him to go on—surely he would have a comment about the neighbourhood or the schools or the tax rates? But he said nothing, and when she looked up at him she realised that he wasn't looking at the book at all.

'You haven't even seen it,' she accused.

'No,' he said. He sounded almost sad. 'All I can see when I'm in the same room is you, Kaye.'

Her heart was tap-dancing to an awkward, amateur rhythm, and her throat was so tight, she thought it would be a miracle if she ever breathed again. His hand brushed her hair with infinite gentleness, almost with reverence, and something deep inside Kaye seemed to shatter like an iridescent soap bubble. It was a bursting so quiet, so infinitesimal, that it seemingly had no meaning at all— except that afterwards, nothing could ever be quite the same again.

She didn't remember moving at all, but she must have, for she was in his arms, pressing herself against him with a mindless abandon, as if she was trying to drown her own identity in his. 'Please,' she whispered, not even knowing what she was saying. 'Please——'

She seemed to be melting, she thought, and felt a sort of vague wonder, but no panic. Brendan guided her towards the blanket in the centre of the floor, and she sank down on to it with relief, sighing with contentment deep in her throat when she was safe in this haven, with him beside her. Suddenly, it seemed, there was no hurry. They were alone, as if they were the only two souls in existence, with the entire universe to be their playground and all of time stretching out before them as the world spun lazily to a standstill...

Brendan seemed to know it, too. He nibbled at her throat, dropping kisses gently on the tender skin. His hand crept up under her loosely knit sweater, over the sensitive skin that stretched taut across her ribs, to the delicate swell of her breast. His touch sent shards of pleasure shivering through her.

Her fingers seemed to have a mind of their own as she unbuttoned his shirt, eager to be rid of the barrier it represented. Her hands wandered over his warm skin, caressing his strong shoulders and pulling him down to her. She was no longer content to wait——

As her hands locked together, the huge emerald on her ring finger cut viciously into her right palm, and she cried out. The pain of the scratch seemed to jolt some sense back into her head, and she stared up at him, horrified.

My God, she thought, have I gone completely insane? A woman who is engaged to one man does not make love on her living-room floor with another one——

'Stop,' she said. Her breath was coming in painful gasps. 'We can't do this.'

'It seems to me that we already are.' He sounded completely out of breath himself. 'I'm not taking the blame for this one,' he said. 'You got yourself into this position, Kaye.'

'I'm not asking you to take the blame,' she whispered. She couldn't look at him. He hadn't moved. His hand was still cupping her breast, and the warmth of his fingers was soaking into her skin.

'You could be called a tease, you know, or worse—for acting like this.'

It was almost accusing, and she shivered a little. She was in real danger, she knew; a wise woman did not lead a man into this sort of excitement and then tell him to stop. If Brendan chose not to listen to her, there would be nothing she could do to resist him. Rape, she told herself, was not a pleasant word, but she knew she had never been closer to it in her life. 'I wouldn't blame you,' she whispered, painfully honest, 'if——'

'Oh, you wouldn't?' he said. 'Thank you for giving me permission to ravish you. You tempt me, Kaye, you really do. But I'm not quite that far gone, and I don't think I'd enjoy having Graham come looking for me with a horsewhip, after you've told him about the nasty things I forced you to do.'

'I have no intention of telling him about any of this.'

'I dare say. But then, you've been known to change your mind before.' He rolled away from her, his fingers lingering against her breast for a long moment. 'You're a damned frustrating woman, Kaye Reardon.'

'You don't understand,' she said. 'I need time to think—— '

'Well, when you've thought, let me know what you decide, will you? By telephone, please—we'll both be a lot safer that way.' He rose in one graceful motion and reached for his necktie.

Kaye scrambled to her feet. She felt as if she'd been thoroughly mauled, and she was glad there wasn't a mirror handy. 'I don't blame you for being angry,' she said. It was such a horribly inadequate thing to say that she was heartily ashamed of herself. Yet what else could she tell him? She could hardly say, I'm sorry I didn't let you make love to me.

But I am, she thought, and the harsh realisation caught at her throat.

He saw the shock of it in her eyes, and he sighed. 'I'm sorry I sounded so crude,' he said. 'I—well, you did give me a jolt, you know. Far more than Omar could have, if he'd chosen to throw a fit. Goodnight, Kaye.'

She followed him to the door. She wanted to remove a loose thread that lay on the lapel of his jacket, but she stopped herself in time. 'Your books——' she said, finally.

He looked at them, spread haphazardly across the couch and the coffee-table. 'I think I'd better get out of here, before I change my mind and make myself at home,' he said. 'I'll pick the books up at the travel agency tomorrow.'

'I won't be there. I'm going out of town.'

He shrugged. 'It doesn't matter. Kaye——' He put out a gentle hand, and drew his fingers down through her hair. It was a tentative gesture, as if he half expected to be slapped. Then he was gone, leaving her standing in the cold breeze.

She stood there for a long time, welcoming the numbing cold because at least it made her feel alive. Finally, however, she closed the door when Omar protested at the draught, and sat down to think. It was past time to be asleep, if she was going to be at the airport at five in the morning. She should unfold the couch and crawl between the sheets right now. But she knew, if she tried to go to bed, that she would not rest.

What was happening to her? She was engaged to a man she was fond of, a man she respected; though she wasn't altogether certain that she loved Graham, she was convinced that blind, head-over-heels love was not always the most important ingredient in a marriage.

And yet, if she was content with her engagement, how could she possibly account for what had happened tonight?

'There is no accounting for it,' she told herself. 'It was temporary insanity.'

But it wasn't the first time it had happened, honesty forced her to admit. Could she promise—as she must, when she married Graham—that it would be the last?

Certainly, she would never again let herself be caught up in that particular form of madness with Brendan McKenna. She would return his books to him as soon as she was back from the Bahamas, and that would be the last time she would ever see him. Graham could do the looking for houses from now on, she told herself. Kaye was disillusioned with the job.

And, since she would never see Brendan again, it followed logically that she would never have to worry about kissing him in the empty, tattered hallway of some old house, or making love with him on a blanket in her own living-room——

But was it really possible, in a town the size of Henderson, to know that she would never run into him again? And even if that could be guaranteed, would her mind be at peace? Or would she walk every day of her life, looking for him in the crowds, searching for him on the city's streets, and swallowing hard each time a black-haired man turned out not to be the one she sought?

She bit her lip as the truth hit her in the face. He had crept into her heart, as Emily had said. Emily had thought Brendan was a passing fancy that, once indulged, would disappear. Kaye wasn't sure it would be so easy to exorcise him from her life.

But she knew one thing. She could not marry Graham. Not now—not while she was carrying this longing for Brendan in her heart.

She put her head down beside Omar on his favourite pillow, and tumbled into sleep.

She almost didn't make it to the airport; if Omar hadn't discovered that his water dish was empty, and let her know about it with a determined and off-key yowl, she would have slept through departure time. In fact, she considered doing that anyway; her bed, after a night spent curled up awkwardly in her clothes, seemed very appealing.

But the pale darkness that was early morning brought with it doubt. Had she really followed it through logically, step by step, last night? Or had she let the emotions of the moment persuade her that she must break her engagement?

'I need some time to think,' she told Omar. And she might as well do that thinking in Nassau, where no telephones, jobs, or visitors could interfere. It would be foolish to do anything else.

She showered and dressed faster than she had ever done before, throwing things into a beach bag almost at random. Then she filled the cat's dishes, kissed him goodbye, and rushed out to her car.

She was fifteen minutes late, but the group of tourists, most carrying tote-bags, others already wearing umbrella hats as if attempting to exert their will over the Midwest's weather, were still milling about the terminal. Kaye rushed up to the grey-haired woman in the purple jacket who seemed to be in charge.

'I'm travelling on Miranda Lilly's ticket,' she explained breathlessly, and handed it over.

The woman looked at her suspiciously over half-glasses, and admitted that she had discussed the matter with Mrs Lilly. 'You're late,' she said.

'Yes, and I'm sorry I overslept. I certainly won't be late the rest of the day, I promise.'

'If you are, you'll be left behind.'

Left behind, Kaye thought. In the Bahamas. She couldn't think of a nicer fate. She snapped back to attention as the woman spoke again.

'I said, do you have a copy of your birth certificate? You'll need it, or a passport, to get back into the country.'

Kaye waved her little blue passport folder under the woman's nose. Marilyn had insisted that she get it when she took the job at Gulliver's, but this was the first time she had ever used it.

'Humph,' the woman said. Her tone seemed to indicate doubt that anyone so unreliable as Kaye could qualify for a legitimate passport. But she couldn't question the official seals, so she put Kaye's name on her list, next to the crossed-off entry for Edward and Miranda Lilly——

That's odd, Kaye thought. But the woman pushed a purple folder into her hands and cleared her throat to get the attention of the group. As she started to give boarding instructions, Kaye began to flip through the information in her folder. Timetable, guide book—it was very thoughtful of them to include that, she thought.

'Hi,' said a husky voice beside her. 'I believe we're seatmates.'

My God, she thought, I'm even hearing his voice, now——

Brendan bent and picked up her beach-bag. 'I'll carry your things on board for you, if you like.'

He was really there, not just a figment of her imagination. Suddenly, Kaye was fiercely, illogically angry, as she saw her vision of a peaceful day on the beach waver and fade. 'Do I have a choice?' she said icily. 'Why in the hell are you here?'

'Because I don't believe in playing fair, when there's something important at stake.'

'Well, you can just go hang.' She grabbed her bag out of his hand. 'I've got one solitary day of vacation time, and you are not going to ruin it for me!'

He looked for an instant as if he'd been slapped. 'I didn't intend to ruin anything,' he said sombrely. 'I thought perhaps we could have a little fun together. We did have fun, you know—at first.'

She felt just a bit ashamed of herself. We had fun, she thought hollowly, until I began to wonder if I wanted more than just fun... 'How did you manage this, anyway?' she asked, a little more calmly. 'You can't expect me to believe you were surprised to see me turn up. But this tour has been sold out for weeks, and I only knew I was coming yesterday.'

'Poor Mr Lilly,' he said mildly, as he followed her up the ramp to the plane. 'Having to stay home and nurse his wife——'

'Emily,' she muttered. 'Damn you, Emily, you set me up! I wouldn't put it past her to have pushed that poor woman down the stairs——'

'Apparently,' Brendan said, 'she set us both up. She seemed to think you would be glad to see me. Obviously she was wrong.' He took her bag and put it in the overhead compartment. 'Window seat? Or do you prefer the aisle?'

'I prefer solitude,' Kaye said nastily.

'Since it's a little late to get off the plane, I suppose you're stuck with me on the trip, but I promise to be very quiet.' He fastened his seatbelt with an emphatic snap. 'You won't even know I'm here.'

Impossible, Kaye thought. How could she not know he was beside her, when every cell tingled at the memory of the way he had kissed her last night? She could still feel the stark demands of her own body, and her longing to let the world be swept away in a rising tide of desire...

'I'm a champion chump, you know,' he said. 'Last night when you said you wanted to think, I actually believed you meant it. But it was really only an excuse to get yourself out of a tight corner, wasn't it, Kaye?'

'I did mean it,' she protested faintly. She had never before heard quite that note of harsh self-deprecation in his voice, and it frightened her.

'One day of fun,' he mused. 'Nothing serious, no discussions, no questions. Just a few hours of adventuring together—that was all I wanted from today. But I promised to be quiet, didn't I? Sorry.'

Why am I so angry? she asked herself. Simply because he had the nerve to intrude on my holiday? But he has every right to be here. It wasn't her own private plane, and he could have bought a ticket, just as all these other people had.

Was she angry at Emily, for the manipulation she had pulled? Yes, she admitted. But that was no reason to be angry with Brendan. Emily hadn't told him the whole story, either.

You're scared, Kaye, she told herself. You're afraid to commit yourself to anything, for fear you'll regret it. Well, he isn't asking for a commitment. He's made it plain that he's only asking for a day to enjoy, together. And you will enjoy it; you do have fun when you're with him. A whole day to play, with no one to intrude——

'Have a fling,' Emily had said. 'Get him out of your system.' Perhaps that was all the day would mean.

But what if this day did not end the madness? What if she wanted more?

No matter what, you will always have today, she told herself firmly. What was it he had said? Something about how memories could never be taken away...

She looked down at her hands clenched in her lap, and realised that she was still wearing Graham's emerald. Brendan knew it, too, she reflected; no one could overlook that ring.

At least have the courage of your convictions, she told herself. You decided last night that no matter what else happened, you couldn't marry Graham. And that hasn't changed.

The jet was taxiing for take-off. It was too late to back out; they were going to Nassau.

You can have a day to remember, she told herself, or a day to regret. It's entirely your choice, Kaye. Which is it to be?

She tugged the ring off. 'Brendan,' she whispered, 'will you take care of this for me today?'

He looked down at the dark green stone, and then into her eyes. 'It's not quite the right thing to wear on the beach.'

'There have been a couple of burglaries in my neighbourhood lately,' she said. 'I could scarcely leave it in the apartment.' Her eyes said much more.

He took the ring, then picked up her hand and pressed his lips to her palm. The tension had melted out of his face.

'My goodness,' said a professionally cheerful voice beside them. 'What a beautiful ring.'

Kaye looked up in surprise at the flight hostess. The young woman smiled and said, 'And what a setting for a proposal. Lucky girl!' She had moved on before Kaye could correct her.

Brendan saw the confusion in her face. 'It isn't important,' he said softly. He wrapped her ring gently in a handkerchief and put it in his pocket. 'Just for today,' he said, 'let's forget about the world.'

You are my world, she wanted to say. But she didn't dare.

CHAPTER TEN

THE jet broke through the clouds just then and sunshine poured in, greeted by applause from the passengers. Kaye turned away from Brendan to stare out the window, and when at last she looked up at him again, her last doubts had vanished. The only thing that mattered was today, she thought; the future would take care of itself. 'Let's forget about the world,' he had said. Very well, she thought. 'No discussions, no quarrels, no questions,' she agreed. 'Just a stolen day of summer.'

He picked up her hand and kissed her fingertips, and the pact was made.

The flight seemed incredibly short, and she was astonished when the seatbelt warning sign came on. A bit later, Brendan cut short her description of Blackbeard's marauding tours through the Caribbean by taking the guide book out of her hands. 'Don't you want to know about the history of the islands?' she protested.

'Wouldn't you rather see them as they are right now?' he countered, and leaned over her to point out the tiny window.

She had scarcely noticed that the plane had been gradually descending, but below them—almost close enough to touch, it seemed—lay a green and white jewel of an island surrounded by a sapphire sea. Foamy white waves rolled lazily toward the beaches and shattered themselves against the sand, withdrawing to regroup and then reach out again. Buildings glistened in the strong sunlight, and palm trees formed a muted green backdrop.

She closed her eyes in sheer delight, and then was almost afraid to open them again for fear it was all just imagination.

It wasn't until the taxi had dropped them in Nassau itself that Kaye allowed herself to believe it was really happening. She stopped in the middle of Bay Street, turned her face up to the sun, drew a breath of pure happiness, and said dreamily, 'I'd love to live where it's summer all the time.'

'How could you appreciate it, if you never had anything to compare it with?' Brendan asked practically. 'And get a hat on—you may adore the sun, but with that fair skin of yours, it isn't going to be very friendly to you.'

'I forgot to bring one.'

'Then shopping is the first order of business.'

'I suppose you'd rather be fishing, like that man you were talking to on the plane.'

'Oh, no,' Brendan said airily. 'Not after everything you told me about the pirates.'

'Are you afraid they're still lurking in the inlets, ready to come and get you? I never dreamed you were a chicken!'

'I'm not. I just think that someone ought to stay around and protect the pirates from you. And if you think that shows a lack of courage——'

'Protect them from me—well!' she spluttered, and he laughed at her, grabbed her hand, and pulled her across to a brightly-painted pushcart where he bought a hand-woven hat and put it on her head himself.

It was a golden day. She stood in the straw market near the waterfront and watched as a woman wove a precious, fine-textured little doll, and then bought it so she would always remember. She was starting to turn away from the little stand when she saw the basket. It was about two feet in diameter, but the pale gold straw was finely woven like that of a much smaller basket, and a dainty pattern in darker straw repeated throughout the delicate work. She had never seen anything quite like it, and Kaye fought a brief battle with her conscience before she bought it. The last thing she needed was another basket. Nevertheless, it would fit nicely in the corner of her apartment, and it would be wonderful to hold all of those magazines that seemed to collect unread, spilling over everything. She gathered up her trophies and turned to look for Brendan.

For a moment, she thought he had disappeared. In his white trousers and brightly printed shirt, he blended right into the rest of the crowd. Then he came towards her from across the market, a silky jade-green scarf fluttering from his fingers. He tied it casually around the crown of her new hat and said, 'There. That should make you easier to keep track of.'

She wrinkled her nose. 'I should think it would be no trouble at all to spot me—just look for the tourist with the palest skin in town. Now you look like a native, at least as far as the costume is concerned. Tell me, did you just happen to have those clothes, or did you have to go shopping?'

His hands were buried in his pockets. 'Oh, these old things?' he drawled. 'One has to have them to go yachting with the boys, don't you know.'

'The trousers, perhaps. But you'd be thrown off any self-respecting yacht in that shirt.'

'Do you insist on having all my secrets revealed? It's a souvenir of a Hawaiian vacation, I'm afraid, and it's one of the calmer ones I own, at that. Are you disappointed?'

'Only mildly. See my new treasure?' She held up the basket.

'I was trying to pretend I didn't see it. Are you really planning to carry that enormous thing around Nassau all day?'

'Oh.' She shifted the weight of her beach-bag and looked down at the bulky basket doubtfully. They had left their coats aboard the plane, but she hadn't considered that she would have to carry her souvenirs until they returned to the airport in late evening. 'Perhaps she'd keep it for me,' she pointed out hopefully. 'The woman who made it, I mean.'

'You might not get back here to pick it up. And don't look at me—I have no plans to haul it around. But if you won't go all Victorian on me, we can rent a hotel room for the day——'

'I have no intention of spending the day in a hotel room.'

'To leave our excess stuff in,' he went on, as if she hadn't interrupted. 'And to change clothes, and a few things like that. Or had you planned to get into your swimsuit right on the beach?'

'I could. I'm wearing it under my clothes.'

'Well, that's handy. But it might be a little less than comfortable on the trip home.'

She had to admit the truth of that. She hadn't been thinking quite clearly enough at five in the morning to have considered all the problems of a trip like this, she decided. 'All right,' she agreed warily. 'A hotel room it is. But I insist on paying my half. It is my basket, after all.' And an expensive souvenir it was turning out to be, she reflected.

'I can't wait to see the desk clerk's face when he hears this one,' Brendan said.

The hotel clerk, however, made no fuss at all; he simply handed over the key with a smile and a pleasant wish for them to enjoy their stay. And any distrust she might have felt about Brendan's motives vanished when he ushered her into the room and promptly disappeared into the bathroom to change into his swimming trunks.

'So much for my maidenly fears of being held captive in a hotel room for the rest of the day,' Kaye mocked herself, as she traded her own street clothes for a terry robe to cover her swimsuit. 'He doesn't want to miss a minute in the sun any more than I do!' Brendan certainly seemed to have no intention of breaking their agreement to discuss nothing serious, or of repeating the craziness that had nearly overcome them both last night in her apartment. And it was really insane, she told herself sternly, to be wondering why, and regretting it.

They swam and played in the waves. 'Too bad we don't have time to learn to scuba dive,' Brendan mused as they lay on the white sand. 'Emily could have been thoughtful enough to let us know we were coming, so we could have prepared ourselves.'

'By taking lessons in Lake Henderson, I suppose,' Kaye said, with a shiver.

He propped himself up on an elbow and looked down at her, and she wondered for one shaky instant if he was going to kiss her. He had that sort of look about him. But he only said, 'In the summer, the lake is perfectly warm. Next time, we'll have to plan ahead.'

'Is there going to be a next time?' she asked, and could have bitten her tongue off. He was certainly keeping his end of the bargain, while she—— 'Sorry,' she muttered. 'We weren't going to discuss that.'

What's the matter with you, Kaye Reardon? she asked herself. It's driving you bananas that he doesn't seem to feel any need to get things hashed out and decided. He's quite willing to have a good time, and let tomorrow worry about itself——

The darkness in his eyes hovered there for another moment, and she sucked in a deep breath of discovery. You want him to be serious, she accused herself. You want things all straightened out and neatly packaged; you want your future wrapped up in pink paper with a guarantee attached. You're not suffering from some mere passing fancy, or infatuation. You've fallen in love with Brendan McKenna, and you want to be his wife...

Well, she told herself, the first step is to tell him about that ring in his pocket at the hotel, and how you're planning to give it back the next time you see Graham. Tell him, Kaye, she ordered herself. Tell him, and then you'll know——

But remember, she reminded herself, that he may not feel the same way you do. You may be certain that you want to marry him, but that doesn't mean that he's going to throw himself at your feet with a proposal. He may not be flattered at the idea that just yesterday you had every intention of marrying Graham, but today it's Brendan you want.

And remember that he's the one who said he didn't want to ruin this day with serious things...

He grinned. 'You're getting pink,' he said. 'One more dip, and then we'll have to get you out of the sun.'

It wasn't the sun, she wanted to tell him. But her nerve had vanished; she didn't have the courage to tell him, and risk the rest of this day. One day of fun...

That was why it had been so much fun to look at houses with him, she thought. Even then, she had been falling in love with him.

They swam some more, and then had a late lunch at a little restaurant near the beach, where most of the diners were dressed as casually as they. They ate fried conch and drank banana rum, and Kaye tried to forget that her island idyll was more than half over. Every time he touched her, no matter how casually, the hunger to be in his arms grew.

In the late afternoon, Brendan dragged her off the beach, despite her protests. 'If you stay out in the sun any longer, you'll be so burned that you won't be able to sit down for days,' he argued. 'We'll have a shower first, and look in on what's happening in one of the casinos, and then we'll find some place quiet to have dinner——'

And then we'll go home. He didn't say it, and she didn't want to think it. But the end of the day hovered over her like a threatening cloud.

She hurried to shampoo the salt water from her hair, unwilling to waste an instant of time. But suddenly it wasn't the island, and the beach, and the city that called to her, but him. It wasn't that she couldn't bear to miss a moment of Nassau, she realised; it was the minutes with Brendan that she didn't want to lose. A sound outside the shower made her jump, and her heart beat a little faster at the idea that he might have come in to join her. But then there was silence again, and she turned the shower spray off and wrapped herself in the thick terry robe so thoughtfully provided by the hotel.

Brendan was lounging on the bed, the pillows piled up behind him, and she stopped in the bathroom door and watched him greedily for a moment, his long legs stretched out, his hands clasped behind his head, the dark blue swimsuit hiding so little of him that he might as well have been stretched out there naked for her inspection.

If Emily were to see him like this, Kaye thought with a sudden dart of humour, she'd say, 'Excuse me, Kaye, but under these circumstances it's every woman for herself,' and she'd attack him.

And just what, Kaye wondered, was holding her back from doing just that? Ladylike restraint? Fear of being rejected? That was a little ridiculous; she'd practically been in bed with him last night, and he'd certainly shown no hesitation then. She'd spent the afternoon hoping that he would stop being such a damned perfect gentleman, but he was only obeying the rules they had agreed to that morning. What if she simply stopped playing by the rules? What better way was there to tell him how much she wanted him?

She was hardly breathing as she walked across the room to him. He looked up as she paused beside the bed, and then she sat down beside him and very deliberately ran one index finger from his throat, where a gold medallion on a chain nestled almost hidden among the dark curls of hair on his chest, to the elastic band of his swimming trunks. Then she leaned forwards and kissed him, slowly, with every ounce of enticing energy she could muster.

His mouth was warm and mobile under hers, and by the time she ended the kiss her head was swimming and her insides had melted into a pool of lava, ready to erupt without thought of consequences, or damage.

'If I didn't know better,' he said in a husky, unsteady voice, 'I'd think I was being treated as a sex object.'

'Would you mind,' she whispered.

'Mind?' It was a drawl now, frankly seductive. 'Honey, I'd be delighted.' He moved a fraction of an inch, and pulled her gently down beside him, into the nest of pillows he had made for himself. She could smell the salt water still on his skin, and something more that was indefinably him, and that she would recognise, she was convinced, at the ends of the earth. Essence of Brendan, she thought muzzily. Bottle it, and women all over the world would buy it for their men...

Her fingers wandered over his body, exploring shyly, tentatively, and then with growing confidence and a sense of delighted wonder as his tightened breathing told her what she was doing to him. Then, suddenly and unaccountably, her plaything growled and twisted out of her grasp, and suddenly she was the aggressor no more. In the abrupt shift of pattern, she found herself the toy as he caressed and cherished her, and she struggled to hold on to sanity and cling to the ever-shifting edge of a world that had suddenly gone quite mad, a world that seemed to fade and ooze and blur...

And then not even the world mattered any more, as he took her over the edge. Reality slipped slowly from her loosened fingers, and the single truth that remained was the man who was her only shelter from the volcano that threatened to consume her alive. She clung to him, pulling him down, begging him with her body not to leave her, never to let her be alone again...

It took a long time after that before she could even breathe normally. She was afraid to look at Brendan; she was vaguely embarrassed to have displayed such shamelessness, and she wasn't sure she wanted to know what he thought about it. He had collapsed next to her, his raspy breathing tickling her throat, as if he never intended to move again.

Eventually he captured her hand and began to kiss each fingertip, slowly and sensually. He was working his way up her arm, pausing at each pulse-point, when she opened her eyes and was shocked to see that dusk had fallen.

'Brendan, what time is it?' she asked in panic. 'We're going to miss the plane!'

He didn't bother to open his eyes. 'The hell with the plane. Let's stay in bed for a couple of days, and then think about going back.'

'We can't be so irresponsible.' She struggled out of his grasp and reached for her wristwatch.

'Why can't we? We were irresponsible enough to come in the first place. I'm sure we can explain it to Marilyn somehow.'

'Marilyn gave me one day off—not the whole week. And it isn't only Marilyn I'm thinking about,' she muttered. She shrugged herself into the terry robe and began frantically throwing things into her bag.

'Well, I don't think there will be people standing in line outside my door. You're my only important client at the moment. Everybody else can wait till next week to buy a house.'

A cold chill settled around her heart. You're my only important client . . . And did that mean she was only important to him as a client? Had nothing changed at all?

Only you, Kaye, she told herself. He's made no promises, asked no questions, arranged no plans. You're the one who's doing the assuming here.

Don't be ridiculous, she told herself. Of course things have changed. He couldn't make love to me like that if I meant nothing to him! If the sale was all that was important to him, he wouldn't have risked it like this—— But it made her feel rather sick even to think about that.

She turned to him, her green eyes pleading. 'Brendan, we don't have time to talk about it now. I have to make that plane.'

His eyes had chilled to blue ice. 'Of course,' he said. 'How foolish of me. It's Graham you're concerned about, and not Marilyn.'

That's not true, she wanted to say. You must know that's not true! But it was, in a way. She wanted to talk to Graham right away, before any gossip could reach him. She didn't want to hurt him any more than she had to.

'Tell me, Kaye,' Brendan asked, 'how are you going to explain this little aberration to Graham?'

She tried to swallow, and couldn't. That actually sounded like a threat, she thought dizzily. Was this the man she thought she loved?

Her nails were cutting into her palms. She didn't look at him. I can't bear to tell him I love him, she was screaming inside, if all I am to him is a client, a source of income to pay for that new car. It would kill me to say that to him, and have him laugh at me——

Her voice was painfully tight as she asked, 'What is there to explain to him?'

Then she held her breath. Please, she begged silently. I've gone as far as I can. You have to talk to me, Brendan. Tell me you care for me. Tell me that you don't want me to marry Graham. Tell me anything at all, even that you don't know what you want right now, that you don't know if we have a future, but you want to find out——

The silence lasted a full minute. Then Brendan rolled off the bed with a single fierce lunge, and Kaye clutched her beach-bag to her breast, as if it might provide a little protection. But he didn't come close to her. Instead, he reached for his street clothes, folded in a neat pile on a chair, and started to get dressed.

'You're quite right,' Brendan said, with a cold certainty that seemed to cut her into slices. 'There's nothing to explain to him. Just a stolen day of summer, I think you called it. He certainly couldn't object to you having a holiday.'

There was a burning ache in her chest, as if her heart had quietly ripped in two. It was an agony too painful for tears to ease; yet, in a way, it hurt less now that she knew for certain where she stood. At least now she wouldn't make a clown of herself any more. He might have used her, and made a fool of her, but at least he couldn't laugh at her folly any more.

In the lift, though, her control snapped. Brendan had hurt her more than any other man had ever begun to, and he deserved a little pain himself, she thought. He deserved to hear the truth. That would be far more painful for him than anything else she could say.

'I ought to marry Graham,' she said, her voice low and bitter. 'At least I know what to expect from him. He's honest and decent, and if I don't exactly love him, at least I can respect him and believe in what he says. He's stable and dependable—he goes to work every day, and he doesn't just fling off for a fishing trip or a day in the Bahamas any time it suits his fancy. What you call your precious independence frightens me, Brendan. It looks like selfishness to me. You're just like my father. You're the only person you care about. You use people and toss them aside. What are you going to do when the fun runs out? It's all very well to be a footloose playboy in your thirties, but your memories won't keep you warm for ever. When are you going to realise that the most lasting things in life take work, and dedication, and sacrifice? I feel sorry for you, Brendan. And I feel sorry for myself. My fiancé is in Colorado making sure his product doesn't hurt the innocent children it's supposed to help, and I'm here having an affair—— '

'Believe me,' Brendan said harshly, 'Graham won't hear about this little romp from me.'

Kaye looked him straight in the eye and struck back, in the only way she knew. 'It never occurred to me that you might tell him. It would ruin your chances of selling a house and getting a commission.'

The instant the sarcastic remark was out of her mouth, she regretted it; if there was one thing Brendan McKenna wasn't, it was money-hungry, and it was a dirty thing to accuse him of. But she hardened her heart and refused to even think of apologising. She didn't regret the other things she had said, and she wasn't about to start telling him she was sorry.

At the hotel entrance they were hailed by a middle-aged couple just getting into a taxi. Brendan's fisherman friend and his wife, Kaye thought. They were late going back as well.

Brendan's hand closed on her arm as if to pull her back into the hotel. Kaye shook him off. 'May we share your taxi?' she called.

'Sure,' the man replied. 'The driver promised to get us to the airport in record time.' He occupied the time by detailing his day's sport to Brendan, who sat across from Kaye and watched her all the way to the airport. She wouldn't look at him. She didn't want to see what might be in his eyes.

Finally, the fisherman's wife sighed. 'I spent the day in the casino on Paradise Island so I wouldn't have to go fishing with him,' she told Kaye, 'and I'd just as soon not hear all about it on the way home, either.'

Kaye nodded her agreement. 'Why don't we swap seat partners on the flight?' she said. Anything would be better than long hours of uncomfortable silence, cramped into the narrow seats of the plane, next to Brendan's body but miles from his soul.

She heard scarcely a word the talkative casino player had to say as the jet arced through the night. Kaye was too busy going back over the day—every phrase, every touch, every gesture—searching for meaning, wondering where she had gone wrong and what she could have done differently. She had been so sure that he must care for her, too. How could she have been so wrong?

'They can't take memories away,' Brendan had said. Too bad, Kaye thought. I'd pay to be rid of this one.

But where, she asked herself helplessly, where did I make the mistake?

Her anger burned itself out somewhere in the darkness over the heart of America, and she began to wish that she hadn't flung those angry words at him. There was truth in what she had said, of course—his independent streak, his unwillingness to be tied down, did frighten her. But not everything she had said was true. He was not like her father, not altogether, and it had been a cruel and hateful accusation to fling at him. He had used her, yes, but had she not used him as well? There was a gentle side to him—a generous and tender side he showed to Nora. Those were things her father had been incapable of feeling.

Why, she wondered painfully, can't I seem to touch that side of him?

When they finally landed at the airport outside Henderson, it was nearly midnight. Kaye struggled off the plane with her beach-bag and her big basket. The shock of the cold March wind outside the terminal, after the glorious sunshine of the Nassau day, nearly took her breath away. She was almost to her car when Brendan called her name.

She spun around, her heart thumping. Had he, too, spent the flight going over each word? Then perhaps there was hope. Perhaps he was coming to tell her that he understood what she had been trying to say, and that he did care after all——

And she knew, with every cell of her body, that if he said a gentle word she would fly to him. She would leave the world behind and count it well lost if she could have him instead. Better a life with him, unpredictable and unsettling as it might be, than the dull serenity of existence without him, if only he cared about her, just a little bit——

But the stern set of his jaw removed any hope from her heart. She looked up at him in silence, and he thrust the emerald ring at her. 'You wouldn't want to explain how you happened to lose this,' he said curtly.

She automatically took it. It was still warm from his hand as she slid it on to her finger. 'No,' she said, honestly. 'I wouldn't. Thank you for keeping it for me today, Brendan.'

He looked at the ring, the outdoor lights reflecting harshly from the green surface of the huge stone. Then he turned, without a word, and strode away across the car park.

She felt as if he had taken her heart with him.

Emily and Marilyn wanted every detail. By noon Kaye's nerves were screaming with the effort of keeping up a bright line of chatter about how wonderful the trip had been, recalling every fragment of the business arrangements for Marilyn's benefit, and not letting slip a hint of the darker side. She studiously avoided the mention of Brendan's name, afraid that her voice alone would give her away.

The only thing that saved her, she thought, was the fact that, with Marilyn there, Emily couldn't ask the questions she really wanted to. Emily was obviously dying to know how her plot had worked out, and Kaye was determined to give her no satisfaction.

No, she admitted, that wasn't quite true. She was afraid of what Emily would say. The last thing she wanted was sympathy, and if Emily gave her any, she would probably melt into a puddle of tears in the middle of the office floor. When Emily went to lunch, Kaye sank into her chair with a thankful sigh. At least she had an hour when no one would be asking difficult questions.

Thirty minutes later, Claudia Forrest came in, and Kaye swallowed a groan. If there was one person she didn't want to talk to right now, before she'd had a chance to give her engagement ring back, it was Graham's mother.

Claudia's bright blue eyes summed up the office. 'Graham's coming home today, and I thought it would be a nice surprise for him if we picked him up at the airport and took him to lunch.'

Kaye closed her eyes momentarily in gratitude that she had the world's best excuse to say no. She couldn't imagine a more uncomfortable afternoon.

Marilyn turned from the filing cabinet where she was putting new guide books in order. 'You can go early, Kaye,' she said generously. 'I'll cover the office till Emily comes back. Take as long as you like.'

That's another person who will be disappointed when my engagement's broken, Kaye thought. But before she could protest, or attempt to explain, she was being bundled out to the car.

The airport terminal was quiet, a considerable change from the night before, when the weary planeload of sun-burned travellers had debarked. She'd been standing just about here, Kaye reflected, when she'd looked up to see Brendan's eyes on her. That was when she had fled out to her car, and he'd caught up to return her ring——

'Kaye,' Claudia said gently.

'I'm sorry. What did you say?'

'That's just it, dear. I haven't said anything for ten minutes, and you didn't even notice.' Then, even more tenderly, she added, 'You don't look like a girl who's anxiously waiting for her fiancé. You're dreading the moment when Graham gets off that plane, aren't you?'

Kaye nodded, wearily.

'I was hoping that the strain between you at brunch that day was only wedding nerves,' Claudia mused. 'You're not going to marry him, are you?'

'No.' It was a painful whisper. 'I don't love him.' Last week, she thought, I'd have said it didn't matter.

'Love,' Claudia said, and Kaye braced herself. But then the older woman surprised her. 'It's so easy to talk yourself into believing that it doesn't matter,' Claudia said softly, 'that other things are more important to the success of a marriage. And in the daylight, it really doesn't make much difference if you love your husband. But in the stillness of the night, Kaye, when the babies are sick, or when you can't sleep and you find yourself lying in the darkness next to a man you sometimes feel you don't even know—then love makes all the difference.'

'You sound as if you know,' Kaye ventured.

'I do. I was a good wife, Kaye, and I don't believe that my husband ever realised that there might be something missing. But I knew.' She rubbed her neck absently, as if it ached. She looked suddenly older. 'I want better than that for my son. I thought perhaps you were it.'

Kaye shook her head. 'I wish I was,' she said honestly, and for a moment she wondered if it might be possible, after all. It would be so much easier to marry Graham than to have to live with the memories of Brendan——

They can't take memories away... Oh, stop it, Kaye told herself fiercely. If you're going to remember every crazy thing he ever said, and repeat it inside your head like a refrain, they'll be hauling you off to a padded cell before the week is out. And who says, anyway, that marrying Graham could make you forget?

'Tell Graham I'm sorry I couldn't stay to meet his plane,' Claudia said. 'I'll take a cab and leave the car for you.'

Kaye rose with her. A dozen things were fluttering through her mind, uppermost among them admiration for the tact this lady displayed in leaving her alone just now. I never thought of her as a real human being before, Kaye thought. It never occurred to me that she had feelings, and tragedies. In the end, she said only, 'Thank you, Claudia.'

On the way back to town, she broke the news to Graham. 'I just don't love you,' she finished honestly. 'Not in the way that I need, in order to marry you.'

'Love can grow,' he reminded.

'Not——' she hesitated. Not when there's someone in the way, she had almost said. 'I don't think it would, in our case.'

'There is someone else.' It was not a question, and before she could say anything, he had taken the next step. 'That estate agent.' She didn't deny it, and a moment later he said, 'I find that very difficult to be-lieve, Kaye. What has he got to offer you?'

'Nothing,' she whispered. Not even the hope of a future, she thought.

Graham sighed. 'I don't suppose there's any point in arguing with you.'

'No.'

'Then I'll just say, best wishes.'

'Thank you for understanding, Graham.' She tugged the emerald ring off her finger and dropped it into his hand.

'I didn't say that I understood,' he pointed out. He sounded a little peevish, as if his pride had been scratched but his heart left untouched. She was glad, suddenly, that she had discovered the truth before she married him. It would have been a disaster for them both.

He parked the car in front of the travel agency and walked her to the door. 'Let me know when the children come, Kaye. I'll send you a case of baby food. You'll need all the help you can get, I'm afraid.'

He sounded like a fretful old uncle, and she burst into half-hysterical laughter and threw her arms around him. 'Thanks, Graham. You're a dear, really you are.'

He looked down at her. 'You would have had everything a woman could want, Kaye.'

'Except love,' she agreed, suddenly sober. 'And if I loved you, and you loved me, that alone would have been enough.' She stood on tiptoe and kissed him goodbye, and then she went back into the travel agency to pick up the disrupted threads of her life. In time, perhaps, she thought, the painful parts of the last few weeks would dim, and she could remember the glorious moments instead. Perhaps. She hoped it would be soon.

CHAPTER ELEVEN

THE week crept by. She didn't exactly expect to hear from Brendan, and he didn't call. And though she would have liked to be brave enough not to care whether she saw him or not, she made a careful survey of the car park at the shopping plaza each day when she went to work, and breathed more easily when she didn't see his car.

It will get easier, she told herself. The time will come when you don't look for him any more, and some day it won't even matter to you when someone talks about him.

But as the days wore on, she found herself regretting more and more the sharp things she had said to him. In the long, lonely evenings at home, she couldn't keep from going over and over that last conversation in her head.

She spent more time that week than she had in years, reflecting on her father, and the things that had made him as he was. He had been a dreamer, an impractical man caught in a prosaic world. Unable to deal with reality, he had fled from it, into one quixotic scheme after another. But never had he set out to hurt anyone. And though Kaye's childhood had been deprived of material things, she had never been denied love.

She could not help but wonder, now that she knew herself how it felt to lose a loved one, how much her mother's death had changed him. Had her mother been the practical one, the person who could have been his anchor? Once he had lost his love, had the rest been preordained?

And what of Kaye herself, and the man she loved? He was quixotic, too. Could she be an anchor for him—or would she ever have the chance to find out? Had the words she flung at him been too much for any man to stomach?

She had been hasty, and she had said things that hurt. But the man had made no move to see her or talk to her. If he cared the least fraction about me, she thought, he would have called. He would have tried to explain——

Or at least he would have stopped by to pick up his damned books, she thought, giving the stack of house-for-sale publications a shove. They were still taking up space on her coffee-table, and every time she looked at them it was like a thorn in her heart, a reminder of the precious hours when she had been certain that she mattered to him.

She tried to feel angry that he hadn't even come to get the books. He must have a horribly guilty conscience, she told herself, if he would actually replace the books rather than face her to retrieve these. But all she could feel was sad.

'It's not crazy to think about him,' she told Omar. 'I didn't imagine all the good things about him—the gentleness, the fun. I accused him of being a playboy, but he wasn't the one who dragged me into bed. He may have taken advantage of me, but I'm the one who gave him the chance. If I had kept my head, we'd have gone to dinner and back to the plane, and we wouldn't have had that argument, and I'd still be seeing him now. Damn it, Omar. Why did I have to be such a fool?'

The cat put his head on her shoulder and purred. At least someone was happy these days, Kaye told herself.

Her words had to have cut Brendan deeply, she thought. She had held Graham up to him as the example of manliness, when she knew, deep in her heart, that a man who put his business first would not make much of a husband. She wanted more than that from the man she loved.

Was it any wonder he hadn't even tried to talk to her? Her accusations had been designed to hurt, and she knew only too well how successful she must have been. Or, she thought, even worse, had what she said not mattered to him at all?

'That's beside the point. I'm going to have to apologise,' she told herself. 'For my own peace of mind, I'll have to tell him I'm sorry for a lot of what I said. Dammit, why couldn't I fall neatly in love with Graham? He thinks the way I do——'

No, he doesn't, she reminded herself. Graham wanted a wife, a house, a family because those things were expected of a man in his position. She closed her eyes and tried to imagine Graham bathing a baby, or soothing a sick child, or listening to a teenager's tale of injustice. He would have no patience to spare for problems like that; those irritations in life would all be delegated to his wife because the smooth running of his home would be strictly her concern. Kaye started to giggle. 'Graham doesn't need a wife,' she said, 'he needs a vice-president!'

Brendan, on the other hand, she thought, would be a different story. Her eyes grew soft at the thought of Brendan's capable, beautiful hands dealing with an infant, just as surely as he had caressed her——

'And that's enough of that,' she reminded herself. Brendan McKenna might never stop moving long enough to find out what fatherhood was like.

But that was really none of her business, Kaye told herself. She could argue with herself till doomsday, but she still had an apology to make. It took her another day to work up her courage, and on Saturday she gathered up his books and took them back to the estate agency.

Cindy, the gorgeous brunette at the front desk, looked quizzically at Kaye, and then at the stack of books she carried.

'These are Brendan's,' Kaye said, in her best brisk and businesslike voice. 'He loaned them to me, and I'm sure he's been anxious to get them back.'

'Oh, there's no hurry.' The girl put her pencil between her teeth so she had both hands free to manage the heavy books. 'I'll put them in his office. Shall I have him call you?'

'He isn't in? I thought I saw his car——' Dummy, Kaye told herself. You worked up your courage and plotted your act all out, but you weren't even smart enough to make sure he was here!

'No. Didn't he tell you?' the girl added indistinctly, around the pencil.

'Tell me what?' Kaye asked. There was a flutter of foreboding deep inside her. What had Brendan done now?

'He's in Wisconsin, fishing, this week. He left Wednesday afternoon—but I was sure he'd told all his clients.'

On Tuesday night, Kaye thought, we were in Nassau. And Wednesday he goes fishing? He certainly didn't waste any time in getting out of here. I wonder if he thought I might get a wrong impression if he stayed around. He might have thought I'd come back and beg for some more of his attention——

So much for the idea that my tirade might have hurt his feelings, she thought. And I believed that he might actually have taken it seriously! I came in to apologise for what I said, and they tell me he was so unconcerned about it that he's already off on another spree! Dear, sweet, selfish Brendan——

She was building up to an explosion, and the girl was watching her curiously. There was no point in making a scene, Kaye decided; Brendan would be certain to hear about that, and her dignity demanded that she not give him the satisfaction. She swallowed her anger and said, civilly, 'I see. I'm no longer looking for a house, so I suppose that's why he didn't bother to let me know he was going out of town.'

The girl set the books on the shelf behind her desk and took the pencil out of her mouth. 'Have you and Mr Forrest found what you were looking for?'

'Not exactly.' Her broken engagement was not a secret, but Kaye could see no reason to confide in Cindy.

'If we can do anything for you——'

'Thank you. I'll keep it in mind.' Kaye started towards the door, and then turned. 'Tell me,' she said. 'I don't mean to be nosy, but doesn't it bother anyone around here when Brendan just takes off like this?'

'Why should it?' the girl asked. 'He sold three million dollars' worth of property last year. If he stayed around all the time, no one else in this office would ever sell anything.'

Kaye blinked. Three million dollars? He had certainly never said anything to her that indicated that sort of volume. But then, she realised, she had never asked, either.

'Real estate is an odd field,' the girl went on. 'You can work like fury and not sell a thing. It's mostly a matter of trusting your instincts and learning to be in the right place, Brendan says. And being patient.'

'Just like fishing,' Kaye said, with wry humour that stopped barely short of bitterness.

'You might say that,' said the girl, thoughtfully. 'Maybe I should learn to fish. It certainly seems to have worked for him.'

Kaye managed to get out of the office without showing her shock. So Brendan wasn't exactly small fry himself, was he?

Not that it mattered, she told herself. He was still irresponsible, no matter how many lucky deals he had pulled off last year. A fishing trip to Wisconsin—in the middle of March, at that. She wondered what on earth he was fishing for. And she hoped he froze his toes off.

Enough, she thought. I've made my effort to apologise, and I'm done. I'm not going to chase after a man who has made it quite plain that he doesn't want anything to do with me. It's time to pick myself up and go on living. I used to be quite happy without him, and I can be again.

Well, she reflected, I won't be exactly happy, perhaps. But I can be content with my life again——

No, I can't, she realised suddenly. Not after he moved in and thoroughly shook it up. If only he wouldn't do that sort of thing all the time, she thought helplessly. Life with him would be something like living on a roller-coaster.

But at least I'd know I was alive, she thought humbly. With him, life would be a heady brew, rich and strong——

But she hadn't been invited to share his life, she reminded herself. And even if there had been a hope of a life that included him, in any way at all, she had sacrificed it when she had flung those flesh-tearing words at him in the hotel lift in Nassau. She would simply have to live with the consequences.

*　　*　　*

She took Nora Farrell to church on Sunday morning, and out to lunch afterwards, ignoring the warnings of her conscience, which said she was doing it for selfish reasons and not humanitarian ones. Why should Nora suffer because Brendan was out of town? she asked herself. If Nora wanted to talk about him, Kaye didn't have to listen.

But Nora didn't mention him, and by the time they were finished with lunch, Kaye's nerves were screaming. Why had Nora been so silent about him, when before he had been her favourite subject? Was she angry at Brendan herself? Or had he asked her not to talk about him to Kaye——

Now you're getting paranoid, Kaye told herself in disgust.

On the way home, Nora asked, diffidently, 'Did Brendan understand when you told him about the key?'

'Key?' Kaye asked absently. Then she caught herself. The key to Nora's house still lay in the bottom of her handbag; it had made the trip to Nassau with her, and she had completely forgotten that she had intended to give it to Brendan.

Nevertheless, she concluded, with her brain working furiously, she didn't dare admit that she still had the key, or Nora would probably ask to be taken to the house right now.

'Of course he understood,' she said. And now, she reminded herself, you're a liar. You'll have to track Brendan down now, just to make sure he doesn't give you away next time he talks to Nora—— Oh, how complicated a life of intrigue can get to be!

'He didn't say anything about it,' Nora said stubbornly.

'I mean, I'm sure that he will understand. I didn't give it to him myself, actually—I left it at his office. But he'd already gone to Wisconsin.' And you, my girl, she told herself, are getting in deeper and deeper.

She dropped Nora off with a thankful sigh and turned towards the supermarket; there were a few things she needed before she went home. Some home, she thought rebelliously. Four walls and a cat, and no future at all.

Your future is what you make it, Kaye, she reminded herself. You can keep on as you are, or you can make some changes. For one thing, she could move. She could afford a larger apartment, in a little nicer neighbourhood; it was just that before, she hadn't wanted to put out the extra money. But if she was going to spend her life alone, she owed it to herself to have a place she liked. The balance in the savings passbook wasn't the only measure of success.

She was a little surprised at the thought. Some of Brendan's philosophy must have rubbed off, she thought. For the first time, she realised that being around him had already changed her. She had never in her life done anything so casually, or on such short notice, as she had since Brendan came into her life. A year ago, she would never have taken the Bahamas jaunt, even if the ticket had been dropped into her hand, because it would have been too sudden, and there would have been too many things that had to be done instead.

Well, she thought, with a bit of humility, perhaps I've gained something from the experience after all.

She found herself in front of Nora's old house, without knowing how she had got there. I wish I could walk through it again, she thought, in daylight, so I could really see it.

At night, all the glass had looked dull and blank, reflecting only the interior emptiness. Today, even though the sun was weak, the outside light pouring through the bevelled and leaded windows would make it look like a different house.

Tell the truth, Kaye, she ordered. You aren't particularly interested in the glass. You want to stand there in the front hall and remember the first time he kissed you!

You have a key, she reminded herself. But if you use it, you'll be trespassing. You've got no possible excuse for being in there.

But who is going to make a fuss? the other half of her mind questioned. The For Sale sign is still on the lawn. The lockbox is still on the front door. No one will ever know you were inside. Take a risk, Kaye. Live a little.

She stood on the pavement with her hands in the pockets of her light jacket. Winter had slipped away in the last few days, and spring had tiptoed in. Their stolen day of summer was already no more than a dream, distant and faded. The only reminder that she had gone with him, had made love with him, was inside her, in this tremulous new desire to stop life from passing her by, to give up the safe path sometimes and strike out across the unmarked wild.

She looked up at the house for a long moment, and then she reached into her handbag for the key.

She wouldn't have been surprised if it hadn't worked at all; it would have been only sensible for the bank to have changed the locks. But the tumblers clicked open almost noiselessly, and the door swung silently open under her hand, almost as if the hinges had been oiled. She stepped across the threshold with her heart in her throat.

She had been right about daylight making a difference. High on the stair landing, the rose window gathered the light and then shattered it into rainbows that cascaded across the falling wallpaper and down the stairs, over the faded roses on the old hall carpet and right to her feet. The sheer loveliness of it caught at her, and she blinked tears away—tears, she told herself, that had nothing to do with the memories of the other time she had stood here, safely sheltered in Brendan's arms.

No wonder that Nora loves this house so, she thought. And what a shame that no one else seemed to see the potential here. Kaye did—but it was out of the question for her to do anything about it. A larger apartment was one thing, but that was a long way from taking on the financial burden of a sixteen-room house in desperate need of restoration.

She tore herself away from the rose window and walked on into the big double parlour, with its golden oak mantel and the huge bay window, and for the first time she noticed the scratching noise that was coming from the back of the house. It had been there all along, she concluded, just at the edge of her consciousness. It must be a branch scraping against the outside wall, driven by the March wind, she decided. But it was awfully loud for a branch. Had another window been broken out?

She reached the kitchen and saw the dark outline of a person silhouetted against the window, and only then did she realise that a prudent woman would have got out while she could. The house, warm and deserted as it was, might have attracted all kinds of intruders, from homeless tramps to neighbourhood kids to criminals in hiding——

Too late for that, she thought. 'What are you doing here?' she challenged.

The man turned, and for an instant she couldn't breathe at all. 'I have a key,' Brendan said quietly. 'What's your excuse?'

'You're in Wisconsin, fishing!' she said idiotically.

'I had to come back some time.' He didn't sound as if it mattered much. 'How did you get in?'

'Nora kept a key. I talked her out of it, so I could give it to you.'

He looked her over unemotionally—the same way, she thought, that he would inspect a cracked wall. 'You obviously weren't expecting to see me when you came in,' he said, finally. 'So what are you doing here?'

'I just came in to look around, all right? Must you be so hateful? If I'd known you were here, I wouldn't have come within a mile of the place.'

'No,' he said, 'I don't suppose you would. You left no doubt about your opinion of me.' He kicked at a piece of fallen plaster; the gritty substance sliding across the flagstone floor made the same scratching sound that had drawn her into the room. He was wearing jeans and a flannel shirt with the sleeves rolled up, she noticed; he looked as if he'd just come in off a lake somewhere.

'Look,' she said, with an effort to be cheerful, 'I was really upset when I said those things, and I was scared to death we were going to miss that plane, and I took it all out on you. It was unfair of me, and——'

'Would it have been so awful?' It was a husky whisper. 'To have been left behind in Nassau?'

It would have been the most beautiful thing in my life, she thought. And I wasn't smart enough to see it, or to trust you. She was trying to gather her courage to tell him that, when he went on, 'That's an unfair question, isn't it? Forget I asked it.'

'I didn't really mean all that stuff,' she said uncertainly. 'About you being irresponsible and selfish, and a playboy, and just like my father...' Her voice trailed off as she saw the angry sparks in his eyes. Dammit, she thought; I'm trying to apologise. Why should that make him angry?

'What happened, Kaye? Did you take a good look in your mirror, and decide that it wasn't smart to throw rocks at others for taking part in the same pastimes you were indulging in?'

'What does that mean?' She was aghast at the suppressed fury in his tone.

'I thought you were misguided, and confused about what you wanted. I never dreamed you could be so cold-bloodedly open about what you were doing.' He sounded bitter. 'You call me a playboy, but at least I wasn't cheating on the person I plan to marry.'

'Graham?' she whispered.

'Do you have another fiancé in the wings?' he mocked. 'So you're going to marry him, Kaye. You'll have your big house and your afternoon bridge clubs and your trips all over the world. I'm sure you'll manage to give him a blonde baby or two to photograph and put on the jar labels, just to keep your position secure. But what are you going to do when all that gets old, Kaye—when you're bored with it all? Don't call me when you want to indulge yourself in an afternoon fling. I'm not proud of my part in what happened.'

'*You're* not proud?' she whispered. 'How do you think I feel?'

'Have you made a full confession to Graham? Or are you afraid to tell him, for fear of losing your comfortable niche in life? I wonder just how much Graham will put up with from you——'

Kaye's temper was at white heat. It was no more than she had expected, to have him fling these hateful things at her. But it hurt, nevertheless. It felt as if his words were tiny razors, each one slicing another fragment from her heart. 'Have you finished?' she demanded.

'Not quite. You accused me of being selfish and using people. I think, myself, that you're the champion when it comes to that sort of thing. You've got the innocent face of an angel, my dear, and underneath it is the scheming heart of a——'

She slapped him, as hard as she could. He didn't even flinch, but the imprint of her hand stood out as clearly on his cheek as if it had been painted there.

'Thank you,' he said. 'It needed only that. You haven't disappointed me yet, though an audience would certainly have improved the dramatic value of the scene.'

Her palm stung from the impact. She clenched her fist in her pocket, trying to hide the pain. But the ache was more in her heart than in her hand. 'It's not true,' she whispered.

'You went straight back to him,' Brendan said. 'After what we shared——'

'What had we shared?' She was almost screaming. 'A quick romp in the sack, which didn't mean a damned thing to you.'

'How in the hell would you know what it meant to me? You wouldn't listen to me—you wouldn't stay there with me——'

'Just what would it have solved if we had spent two more days in bed? And as for me going straight back to Graham, look at yourself, Brendan. The whole thing was so unimportant to you that you went fishing in Wisconsin!'

'I did a whole lot more thinking than fishing. And I didn't go fishing immediately.'

For the life of her, she couldn't understand why that had anything to do with it. 'It doesn't matter when you went. You can't make me believe that you were desperate to talk to me when you didn't even stick around and dial a telephone——'

'What point was there in that? You'd made your choice.' He rubbed a hand across the back of his head.

It left a streak of plaster dust across his dark hair. 'What a fool I was,' he said, 'to think that any ordinary guy could take you away from Graham Forrest. But I thought I could. It was pretty conceited of me, wasn't it, to believe that in the end you would prefer me to Graham and his millions?'

'What?' It was a bare whisper.

'You must have found it very amusing,' he said harshly. 'You see, I thought you really were the innocent and lovely girl you seemed to be. I believed you were only engaged to Graham because you'd never really understood what love could be, and I was arrogant enough to think that I might be the man to show you.'

But you did, she thought, and tried to speak. Her throat was too stiff to form the words, and he went on relentlessly.

'Graham was stiff competition, and I didn't think you'd believe me if I told you I'd fallen in love with you over a reuben sandwich at the Wolfpack.'

She made a sound that was something like a harsh croak.

'I didn't recognise it, then, of course. I didn't know it till the day you and Graham came to look at that house in Henderson Heights, and you were wearing his ring. You called me a damn fool that day—do you remember?'

She nodded.

'I was, Kaye. I looked at you, and at that ring, and I knew that if I stood aside and let you marry him, I would never have a day's peace again. But what was there for me to do? How the hell could I make you believe I was what you really wanted? You would have laughed at me if I'd said it. The only thing I could do was make you question your engagement, in the hope that some day you'd turn to me.'

She was trembling. She reached out carefully to the wall and put a hand against it, and then was afraid that the vibrations of her body might knock it down.

'That day you came running to me here, I thought you'd seen what I was trying to show you—that you could never be happy with Graham. But then, when I kissed you, you backed away, and I knew I'd gone too fast. I was afraid that I'd blown everything, and afraid that the reaction would send you straight to him.'

She put her hands to her cheeks. Her fingers were icy against the hot blood pounding in her face.

'So I was back to walking the tightrope again, and I knew that I had very little time. The moment you found a house you liked, there would be no stopping you——' He broke off and looked at her with anger in his eyes. Anger, and sadness, too. 'I was a fool, wasn't I, Kaye? Tell me, did it amuse you? Did you know what was going through my mind?'

She shook her head numbly.

'That day in Nassau when you came to me, I thought you had realised that you could never love Graham. But then you announced that you were going back to him.'

'I didn't say anything of the sort,' she protested automatically.

He didn't seem to hear. 'I still didn't believe that you were capable of cold-bloodedly seducing me—I tried to believe that you were just confused, and frightened of making a mistake. I knew that security was important to you, and you certainly made it plain what you thought of me, and my way of life.'

She tried to swallow, and couldn't.

'And then I remembered what you'd said, and it gave me hope. You said, "I *ought* to marry Graham." I thought that must mean that you knew you shouldn't—

and that you just needed a little space, and some time to think it over.'

She had said that. She remembered it now.

'So I stayed away from you the day after we came back, and I did some planning of my own—how to convince you that I'm not as unsettled as you seemed to believe, and that you wouldn't be spending your life being dragged from one place to the next if you married me——'

She gasped a little, and whispered, 'Why didn't you tell me? Why did you go away, instead?'

'I was on my way over to the travel agency to talk to you, and I was planning to stand on the pavement and shout if I had to, to get your attention. But just then you and Graham drove up in his car, and the two of you stood there on the pavement——'

She closed her eyes in pain, remembering just how they had expressed that final goodbye. 'You saw that?' she whispered.

'Half of Henderson saw it. And only then did I realise what an utter, stupid fool I had been, to ever dream that you might give up that brand of security for me.' He scowled, and kicked at the plaster again, and didn't see the dawning glory in her eyes.

The same sort of stupid fool I was, she thought, not to know that you were incapable of using me and throwing me aside. The same sort of stupid fool who never dreamed you might feel inferior to Graham, and threatened by his very presence—because I saw you as so much more than he ever could be——

'I didn't go back to Graham,' she said.

There was the briefest possible instant of silence. 'Didn't he like your explanation?'

'I gave him his ring back that day——'

'Of course you did,' he agreed. 'A girl always gives a man's ring back, and then throws her arms around him and kisses him goodbye——'

'I don't know about other girls,' she said. 'But that's exactly what I did.'

'And what happened to make you change your mind?'

She swallowed hard, and then she said, very quietly, 'You happened, Brendan.'

He looked down at her with the coldness of pain still in his eyes, and Kaye knew that the rest of their lives might well depend on what she said next.

'I've had a taste of living now,' she said. 'You've showed me that today is the only thing I can count on, that it's fine to plan for the future, but we have to live today.'

He hadn't moved. She swallowed hard and went on, feeling as if she was fighting for her life. 'I love you, don't you see? If I can't have you, then today isn't worth much, and there's no hope at all for tomorrow. I want to spend my todays with you, Brendan. All of my todays.'

Still, he didn't speak, and she felt sanity slipping away from her. It can't be too late, she thought frantically. But what can I say, what can I do to make him believe?

She said, softly, 'Graham will be disappointed if you don't make an honest woman of me, Brendan. He said I'd need all the help I can get, married to you, so he promised me a case of baby food as a gift for each of our children——' The tightness in her throat grew. 'He guessed how I felt about you. And it was such a grand gesture, coming from him, that I just had to hug him——'

'Damn Graham Forrest,' Brendan said, 'We'll buy our own baby food. Kaye——'

She flung herself into his arms with a glad little sob, and he kissed her hard, like a man granted a reprieve at the very foot of the gallows steps. My God, she thought, how close we've come to disaster because we were afraid to admit the truth—afraid that we'd look like fools!

'I won't lie to you, Kaye. I don't have Graham's resources, and the first thing you learn when you go into the property business is not to count your money till it's in your hand. Commissions sometimes vanish into the mist——'

'Like when clients decide not to get married after all?' What a delicious trembling feeling it was, to be free to tease him again! 'Which reminds me, how are we going to pay for the car?'

'It's paid for. You can't still think that I planned to buy it with Graham's money.'

'A good thing you didn't,' she said.

'It tends to be a feast-or-famine kind of living. But I swear we'll always have jam, as well as bread and butter——'

Did the man remember everything she had ever said to him? Kaye wondered, and made a fresh resolve to never attempt to hide the truth from him again. 'You're all the jam I need,' she said, and he pulled her close again. 'Tell the truth, Brendan,' she went on. 'Were you really trying as hard as you could to find a house for me?'

He laughed a little. 'Cross my heart, my love, I worked the hardest for you that I've ever done.'

'Really?' She was vaguely disappointed.

'Yes. Keeping you from liking some of those houses was the biggest challenge I've ever faced.'

She uttered a furious little cry, and he said, 'Would you rather I'd have sold you the one in Henderson Heights? I could have. Graham could have been persuaded to buy it.'

'I would never have forgiven you.' She put her head down on his shoulder and decided that she'd rather not move ever again. But there was something about Nora's kitchen that nagged at the corners of her mind, and finally, she could stand it no more. 'There is a broom and a dustbin in here,' she pointed out.

'That's right.'

'Why are you cleaning up the fallen plaster in Nora's kitchen?'

'Because it kept my hands busy and prevented me from setting the damned thing on fire.'

His hands were plenty busy now, she thought, and sighed in pleasure at the sensation of strong fingers sliding up under her jacket to massage her spine. 'Arson doesn't sound like you,' she said carefully. 'Why would you want to burn this house?'

'Because, regardless of what you think of me, I don't always just think of today. And all I could see ahead of me was a succession of endless years alone, of walking through these rooms and seeing you in every corner, in every beam of light——' His arms tightened around her. 'You see, I couldn't think of a better way to show you that I was deadly serious about you—so I bought your house the morning after we came back from Nassau.'

'That was pretty crazy,' she pointed out gently. It was all she could do to keep from screaming out the gladness in her heart.

'I know it was crazy, but I didn't come to my senses until after I'd signed the papers. Then I saw you with Graham and all I could think of was how glad I was that you would never share it with him. But today— well, today it all seemed like a little too much.'

'Any house would have done, Brendan. Home isn't a place—— '

'Nevertheless, I now own a house. The bank was so anxious to get rid of it that they rushed the paperwork through in record time. So if you've decided you don't like this house after all, then I don't know what we're going to do, because no one else on the face of the earth wants it and——'

'There's always arson,' she said. 'But that wouldn't make Nora very happy.'

'Besides, I'd still have the mortgage hanging over my head.'

'Our heads,' she corrected. 'And as long as we're talking about Nora—shall we ask her to come and live with us?'

He pushed a loose strand of blonde hair behind her ear and looked down at her with deadly seriousness in his eyes. 'Kaye, are you sure this is what you want?'

'Not this,' she corrected. 'You. Wherever you are, and whatever you're doing. That's everything I want.'

His arms tightened around her, and Kaye knew, with a deep conviction that she could feel all the way to her toes, that this was right. This was where she belonged.

She looked up at him with a half-teasing glint in her eyes. 'Hi, honey,' she said, very softly. 'I'm home.'

HARLEQUIN
Romance

Coming Next Month

#3013 THE MARRYING GAME Lindsay Armstrong
Kirra's encounter with Matt Remington on a deserted beach is an episode she
wants to forget. Then she learns Matt is the only one who can save her
father's business—and only she can pay the price!

#3014 LOVING DECEIVER Katherine Arthur
Theresa would have preferred never to see scriptwriter Luke Thorndike again,
let alone travel to New Orleans with him. Yet, although he'd hurt her badly
five years ago, she just couldn't desert him now, when his life was in
danger....

#3015 UNDER A SUMMER SUN Samantha Day
Anne is puzzled by Rob MacNeil's antagonism. After all, he's the interloper,
taking the very piece of land that Anne had hoped to build on. She soon
discovers that Rob is intruding on more than her land....

#3016 A PERFECT BEAST Kay Gregory
Rosemary's enjoyment in teaching is changed when sixteen-year-old Tamsin
acts up. But the sparks that fly between Tamsin and Rosemary are nothing
compared to those touched off by Rosemary's first meeting with Tamsin's
father—the impossible Jonathan Riordan.

#3017 TROUBLEMAKER Madeleine Ker
Ginny was Ryan Savage's sweetheart when he was Grantly's teenage rebel,
before he took off for big-city life. When he comes back five years later,
Ginny, now engaged to an older, more responsible man, wonders what trouble
he'll bring.

#3018 UNWILLING WOMAN Sue Peters
"Just elope," Jess had suggested jokingly to the young woman who didn't
want to marry Max Beaumont—only to soon find herself trapped into
becoming the unwilling Lady Blythe, wife of the arrogant but all-too-
attractive Max....

Available in November wherever paperback books are sold, or
through Harlequin Reader Service:

In the U.S.
901 Fuhrmann Blvd.
P.O. Box 1397
Buffalo, N.Y. 14240-1397

In Canada
P.O. Box 603
Fort Erie, Ontario
L2A 5X3

Especially for you, Christmas from
HARLEQUIN HISTORICALS

An enchanting collection of three Christmas
stories by some of your favorite authors captures
the spirit of the season in the 1800s

TUMBLEWEED CHRISTMAS by Kristin James

A "Bah, humbug" Texas rancher meets his match in his
new housekeeper, a woman determined to bring the spirit
of a Tumbleweed Christmas into his life—and love into
his heart.

A CINDERELLA CHRISTMAS by Lucy Elliot

The perfect granddaughter, sister and aunt, Mary Hillyer
seemed destined for spinsterhood until Jack Gates arrived
to discover a woman with dreams and passions that were
meant to be shared during a Cinderella Christmas.

HOME FOR CHRISTMAS
by Heather Graham Pozzessere

The magic of the season brings peace Home For
Christmas when a Yankee captain and a Southern heiress
fall in love during the Civil War.

Have You Ever Wondered If You Could Write A Harlequin Novel?

Here's great news—Harlequin is offering a series of cassette tapes to help you do just that. Written by Harlequin editors, these tapes give practical advice on how to make your characters—and your story—come alive. There's a tape for each contemporary romance series Harlequin publishes.

Mail order only

All sales final

**A distinctive romance chosen
to salute Penny Jordan fans**

Harlequin Presents...

PENNY JORDAN

lovers touch

Harlequin is pleased to present this special
Penny Jordan title guaranteed to capture
your heart and enchant you as only Penny
Jordan can. *Lovers Touch* is specially selected
to receive the November Award of Excellence,
an honor reserved for your favorite authors.

Look for Harlequin Presents #1216,
Lovers Touch, and the special Award
of Excellence seal of approval
wherever Harlequin books
are sold.

Indulge a Little, Give a Lot

To receive your free gift send us the required number of proofs-of-purchase from any specially marked "Indulge A Little" Harlequin or Silhouette book with the Offer Certificate properly completed, plus a cheque or money order (do not send cash) to cover postage and handling payable to Harlequin/Silhouette "Indulge A Little, Give A Lot" Offer. We will send you the specified gift.

Mail-in-Offer

OFFER CERTIFICATE

Item:	A. Collector's Doll	B. Soaps in a Basket	C. Potpourri Sachet	D. Scented Hangers
# of Proofs-of-Purchase	18	12	6	4
Postage & Handling	$3.25	$2.75	$2.25	$2.00
Check One				

Name _____

Address _____ Apt. # _____

City _____ State _____ Zip _____

ONE PROOF OF PURCHASE

To collect your free gift by mail you must include the necessary number of proofs-of-purchase plus postage and handling with offer certificate.

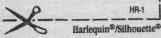

HR-1

Harlequin®/Silhouette®

Mail this certificate, designated number of proofs-of-purchase and check or money order for postage and handling to:

INDULGE A LITTLE
P.O. Box 9055 Buffalo, N.Y. 14269-9055